D0404474

Other Manny Rivera Mysteries by Rich Curtin:

Artifacts of Death

Trails of Deception

MoonShadow Murder

Deadly Games

Death Saint

The Shaman's Secret

Author's Website:
www.richcurtinnovels.com

FEBRUARY'S FILES

A MANNY RIVERA MYSTERY

RICH CURTIN

ISBN: 1469908697
ISBN-13: 9781469908694
Library of Congress Control Number: 2012900859
CreateSpace, North Charleston, South Carolina

Printed in the United States of America

FEBRUARY'S FILES

1

SHERIFF LEROY BRADSHAW STOOD amid the blackbrush and junipers on the high-desert landscape which sloped downward toward the rim of Labyrinth Canyon. He stared at the skeletal hand protruding from the rocks. It looked to him like a body had been shoved under a stone ledge and then concealed by stacking rocks across the opening. He hooked his thumbs in his trouser pockets and wondered how long the corpse had been buried here, out in the middle of nowhere. He also wondered if he was looking at a crime scene or just some hippie burial site.

Dave Tibbetts, a recently-hired young deputy and new to the southeast Utah canyon country, knelt in front of the makeshift grave and took photographs with a digital camera. He worked diligently under the watchful eye of the sheriff while Dr. Pudge Devlin, part-time Medical Examiner for the Moab area, sat on a nearby rock and waited.

"Dave, be sure and get some close-ups of the hand," said Bradshaw.

"Okay, Sheriff."

When the photo session was completed, Bradshaw instructed his deputy to begin carefully removing the rocks one at a time. "Move them downslope about ten feet so the mortuary people have plenty of room to extract the body."

Tibbetts grasped the first rock, a large one, and grunted as he moved it away from the grave. As he continued moving the rocks, some small and some large, more and more of the corpse came into view. It looked like it had been pushed unceremoniously into the opening facing inward with its legs folded at the hips and knees. Small desert creatures had eaten away most of the flesh so there wasn't much left except bones, hair, small patches of mummified skin on the skull, and ragged clothing.

Devlin stood up and walked over to Bradshaw. "If you have to die, it's not a bad place to be buried. Look at the view."

Bradshaw turned around and scanned the landscape. In the immediate foreground was Labyrinth Canyon whose red rock walls channeled the Green River flowing some eight-hundred feet below. Across the canyon, undulating brush-covered mesa land, now golden-grey from the cool October nights, extended westward for thirty miles. Beyond that, mountains, cliffs, and buttes decorated the horizon.

"Yeah, this is gorgeous country. If you like solitude, this is one of the best spots in the county. Not many people come out this way. The two-track road leading out here is pretty hard to find. And if they can find it, it's a long rough ride."

With the last rock removed and the corpse now fully exposed, Tibbetts retrieved the camera and took another series of photographs. Then he stepped aside to make room for Devlin.

Bradshaw watched as Devlin knelt on one knee in front of the grave and silently studied the corpse. It was a beautiful Sunday afternoon in mid-October with clear blue skies and a gentle breeze. Bradshaw had planned to attend the art exhibit at the Moab Arts and Recreation Center this afternoon with his wife Jill. Today had been one of those rare days when the pain of her progressing cancer had subsided, and she'd wanted to get out of the house. Then his cell phone rang. It was his dispatcher. Three young men on ATVs had been exploring the Labyrinth Canyon rims on the east side of the Green River. They'd dismounted to walk to the edge and look down at the river flowing below. One of them spotted an exceptionally large collared lizard scampering across the rocks and through the blackbrush. He gave chase just for the fun of it. The lizard sprinted around a sandstone outcropping and disappeared into a pile of rocks under a cap rock overhang. The rocks looked like they'd been stacked neatly to form a wall. Curious, he removed a few of the rocks to see what was behind them and exposed the skeletal hand. The boys returned to a point where there was cell phone coverage and called the authorities. Now Bradshaw waited to discover whether or not he had a capital crime on his hands.

Devlin examined the corpse for several minutes. Finally he spoke. "Male, late fifties or early sixties. I'd say he was killed about three years ago."

"Killed?" asked Bradshaw.

"There's a quarter-inch hole in the back of the skull. It looks like he was shot with a small caliber weapon." Devlin stood up and dusted off his pants. "I'll know more after we get him back to town where I can do a full autopsy."

Now it was Bradshaw's turn to inspect the corpse. He knelt and ran his hand across the victim's clothing, patting the pockets. He pulled a wallet out of the man's jeans. He opened it and studied the driver's license. "Well I'll be damned. This is February Flanagan. He disappeared from Moab a few years ago. Everyone figured he'd just left town."

"I remember him," said Devlin. "He was a retired newspaper journalist from back east somewhere. New York, I think. Interesting guy. From what I remember, he came to Moab to retire but never could shut off his investigative drive. He started looking for corruption in our little corner of the world. As far as I know, he never found anything."

Bradshaw nodded. "Maybe," he said.

2

DEPUTY SHERIFF MANNY RIVERA parked his Sheriff's Department Ford F-150 four-wheel-drive pickup truck across the street from the Grand County Sheriff's Department building and walked toward the entrance. He was relaxed and in a good mood after his short vacation, and today promised to be another beautiful day. The sun had just risen above the LaSal Mountains to the east and the town of Moab was warming up under a blue sky. The memory of his three-day camping trip with Vivian Ramos was fresh in his mind and produced a hint of a smile on his face. He pulled open the door of the one-story building and strode across the lobby toward his office.

Millie Ives, who had been the sheriff's dispatcher for twenty-one years and who knew pretty much everything worth knowing in the county, looked up from her workstation as he went by. She peered at him over her granny glasses. "Good morning, Manny. How was your camping trip with Vivian?"

Rivera stopped for a moment and looked at her. She was grinning. There were no secrets in this town, he thought. Might as well get used to it. "It was great. Perfect weather. We camped at the Maze Overlook from Friday to Sunday. Took a day-hike down into the Maze. It was incredible. Those canyons go on forever. We want to go back and explore it some more. Got back late last night."

"Sheriff's been waiting for you. He needs to talk to you right away."

Rivera looked at his watch. He was fifteen minutes late, not a good start for a Monday morning, and not typical for him. He stopped at his office and tossed his tan cowboy hat on top of the file cabinet. He went down the hallway to Sheriff Bradshaw's office and knocked on the open door.

Bradshaw looked up from the file on his desk. "Come in, Manny. Grab some coffee and have a seat." He gestured toward the coffee maker on the small table against the office wall. Rivera picked up a white mug with a Kokopelli design and filled it. He sat down in one of the padded leather chairs in front of the sheriff's walnut desk and took a sip. He thought about asking the sheriff how his wife was feeling but decided the question would be pointless. Why remind Bradshaw his wife was slowly dying? Instead he waited for Bradshaw to speak.

"So how was the camping trip?"

"Just fine, sir. Enjoyed it." Rivera could tell from Bradshaw's tone that he had something more important on his mind.

The sheriff's chair squeaked as he leaned back and folded his hands across his stomach. He was a large man in his mid-fifties with receding blond hair combed straight back, an oval face, and light blue eyes.

"A corpse was discovered yesterday by three young men riding ATVs near a bluff overlooking Labyrinth Canyon. You know where that is?"

Rivera nodded. "On the Green River."

"Right. They called it in on their cell phone. I went out there myself with Dave Tibbetts and Dr. Devlin. There was a skeletal hand protruding from a pile of rocks stacked in front of a cap rock overhang. We documented the crime scene, removed the rocks, and uncovered the skeletal remains of a corpse. Nothing left but bone, hair, and clothing. Pudge gave us a preliminary opinion at the scene. Estimated time of death was three years ago, give or take. A single bullet to the back of the head appeared to be the cause of death. The victim's billfold contained over two hundred dollars, so the motive wasn't robbery. According to the driver's license, the corpse was February Flanagan. From Moab. Did you know him?"

"I've heard his name a time or two but I'd never met him."

"I remember him. Interesting guy. Full of stories. Drank a lot. He was from New York. He was killed sometime around his sixty-third birthday. His widow lives on East 300 North. She's been informed. I've notified Adam Dunne at the Bureau of Land Management since the body was found on BLM land." He closed the case file and handed it across the desk to Rivera. "I want you to handle the investigation."

"Yes, sir." Rivera took the file, got up, and headed toward the doorway.

"Oh, and one more thing, Manny."

Rivera stopped and looked back.

"I don't have to tell you how incidents like this can dampen tourism. You remember the killings last year related to that cave full of Indian artifacts. Tourism dropped off noticeably until the case was resolved. Word has spread quickly about the Flanagan murder. People are upset. The business community is already putting pressure on our council members and they've started calling me. Very understandable when you consider that tourism is Moab's entire economy. So get right on this. Keep me informed and let me know if you need any help."

Rivera closed his office door and sat down at his desk. Since the Sheriff's Department had moved from the County Courthouse building to the old Library Building, he now had a slightly larger office and, more importantly, a window through which he could see three peaks of the LaSal Mountains. He'd arranged the office furniture so that he was facing the window with the door on his right. His degree in criminal justice from New Mexico State University in Las Cruces hung behind his desk in a black wood frame. He'd mounted a small Navajo rug on one of the walls, and, since the office had a set of bookshelves, he now had a place to put framed photographs of his parents, grandparents, brothers, and sisters. Rivera was part of a close-knit family. He missed them all dearly since leaving Las Cruces, but the lure of the red rock canyon country around Moab had been strong and addictive. The photographs, in a sense, kept his family members nearby. He'd wanted to add a picture of Vivian as well but wasn't quite sure their relationship had progressed to that stage.

He opened the thin case file and spread the contents out on his desk. There were crime scene reports from Bradshaw and Tibbetts, a map showing the location of the burial site, photos taken during the exhumation, and a preliminary autopsy statement from Devlin. The file also contained the name, address, and phone number of Flanagan's widow. There wasn't much information beyond what the sheriff had already told him.

Rivera picked up the telephone and called the widow. He voiced his condolences and made an appointment to visit her after lunch. During their brief conversation, he'd gotten the impression she wasn't all that forlorn.

He scooped up the paperwork from his desk and placed it back in the file, just as Adam Dunne, the Investigative Agent for the BLM, opened his door and stuck his head into the office. They'd worked several cases together over the past three years and had become good friends. Dunne had responsibility for crimes committed on BLM land in southeast Utah, some of the most rugged country in North America, and more land than any one man or even thirty men could cover effectively. When they'd first met, Dunne had explained to Rivera that Grand County was larger than Rhode Island and Delaware put together, and San Juan County was nearly the size of New Jersey. And those were just two of the counties in Dunne's jurisdiction. So in capital crime cases, he usually played an assisting role with one of the sheriffs' offices in his territory taking the lead. Dunne was wearing a big smile as he slid into one of Rivera's visitor's chairs.

"I hear you've been assigned the Flanagan case."

Rivera looked at him with mock astonishment. "Gosh, Adam, how did you know? I just found out myself."

"News travels fast in a small town, Manny. A big-city boy from Las Cruces like yourself wouldn't understand that."

Rivera smiled. "Looks like once again I'll be doing your work for you, Adam. The body was found on BLM land."

"Appreciate the help, Manny. And don't worry, I'll be there to show you the way whenever you get that bewildered look on your face. Like the one you were wearing when I walked into your office."

Rivera laughed. "So how's the family doing, Adam?"

"Everyone's fine. Ruth is in the first grade now. She thinks she's running the place. Keeps the other kids organized. I think she's destined for management. And Mollie told me last week our fifth child is on the way."

"Congratulations."

"Thanks." Dunne's face now assumed an all-knowing expression. "And by the way, isn't it about time for you to start a family, Manny? You're what, thirty-three years old now? Time waits for no man."

"We'll see." Rivera knew he was hinting about Vivian. Everyone seemed to know his business. "I just read through the Flanagan case file. There's not much here to go on. Did you know Flanagan?"

"I knew him to say hello to, that's about all. He seemed like a nice fellow."

"Do you know if he had any close friends in town? I need to find out more about him. His activities, interests, background, so forth."

"He used to hang around with Wendell Cosgrove, the artist. You know Wendell. He's got his paintings displayed in several of the art galleries around town. Sculptures too. The two of them were big drinking buddies. Wendell could probably tell you a lot about him. I believe the Moab Tavern was one of their regular hangouts."

"Sure, I know Wendell. I'll visit with him later today. Anything else you can tell me?"

"I just came from the hospital morgue. Pudge is doing a full autopsy now. Single shot to the back of the head. Twenty-five caliber. The exhumation team found the slug lying loose inside the skull." Dunne glanced toward the open door, then lowered his voice.

"Pudge told me there was a lot more to this crime than just a bullet to the head."

3

RIVERA LOOKED AT HIS WATCH. It was ten-fifty in the morning and already he was hungry for lunch. He'd gotten up later than usual this morning and had to forego his daily breakfast of sausage and eggs at the Rim Rock Diner. The bowl of raisin bran he'd eaten before leaving home wasn't getting the job done. He decided a cheeseburger and fries would be the next order of business.

He left the building, hopped into his pickup, and drove to Main Street. As he waited at a traffic light, he surveyed the scene. The Moab Rim escarpment to the west was glowing a bright copper color as it did each morning when the rising sun highlighted its east-facing cliffs. The streets were crowded with vehicles, many of them with out-of-state license plates. It was the peak of the tourist season. The community was buzzing with activity as adventure seekers left town headed for the surrounding canyon country in Jeeps loaded with mountain bikes, kayaks, climbing gear, and backpacks. But not everyone came to Moab in search of adventure.

Some came simply to enjoy the sunny days, cool nights, and dry climate of the high desert. There were dozens of shops, restaurants, and art galleries in town. Concerts, lectures, and plays took place most every night. And many of the beautiful geologic formations of Arches National Park and Canyonlands National Park were easily accessible on paved roads. One need not be a rock climber to enjoy Moab.

The light changed to green. Rivera turned left and drove three blocks to the Moab Tavern. The establishment was popular with tourists and locals because it served some of the best food in town and the bar in back of the restaurant was a favorite watering hole. While waiting for his lunch to be served, Rivera wandered into the bar. It was unoccupied except for Stan, the bartender. He was on a stepladder wiping the large mirror behind the bar with a rag.

"Howdy, Stan. Looks like a slow day."

"Hi, Manny. Yeah, on a day like this, most everyone's out in the backcountry. Tonight, the place'll be packed." He stepped down and tossed the rag on the bar. "Can I get you something?"

"No, thanks, but I've got a couple of questions for you."

"Sure. Shoot."

"Did February Flanagan ever come in here?"

"Yeah. Quite often. Feb liked to drink. Mostly Jim Beam. This was one of his regular hangouts. It was only three blocks from his house, so he'd walk over here four or five times a week and spend the evening. Damn shame about him getting shot. Don't know why anybody would want to hurt him." He grabbed the rag and started aimlessly wiping the bar. "He was one of the nicest guys you'll ever meet."

"When he was in here, did he drink alone?"

"Sometimes alone. Sometimes with Wendell Cosgrove. They were good friends. They had fun together, telling stories, kidding each other, laughing a lot. When the Knicks played the Jazz on TV, the place got pretty raucous. The bar would be full of Jazz fans and Feb would be the lone Knicks fan. He was from New York City. He took a lot of abuse during those games, but he loved the camaraderie. He used to say, 'What's the point of being a fan if you're not vociferous about it.' I miss him. Sometimes when he was in the bar and no one else was around, we'd talk about serious subjects. The problems of the world and so forth. He was a very intelligent guy, a deep thinker. Anyway, one day he quit coming. I figured he'd just up and left town. I don't think he and his wife were getting along."

Back at the office, Rivera entered the evidence locker to get a firsthand look at the items removed from Flanagan's corpse. He emptied a cardboard box containing Flanagan's effects onto a metal table. Besides the clothing and shoes, there was a clear plastic bag containing a twenty-five-caliber slug, its front end flattened. There was also a billfold, a plain Wittnauer wristwatch with a faded black leather band, a white handkerchief, three keys on a ring, two hundred thirteen dollars in bills, and forty-six cents in coins. From the billfold he removed a Utah driver's license, a medical insurance card, a plastic card containing the 2008-2009 schedule for the New York Knicks, an ATM card, and a Visa credit card. Nothing unusual.

He returned to his office, sat down at his computer, and checked February Flanagan and his wife for wants and warrants. As expected, both had clean records. He initiated the process for obtaining copies of the credit and debit card statements for the twelve-month period prior to Flanagan's death. He did the same for Flanagan's household telephone records.

That done, he left the building and drove the four short blocks to the Benson residence. He parked his unit in the shade of one of the large cottonwood trees that lined the street. The Benson home was a modest light-blue clapboard structure with white trim around the door and windows.

The doorbell produced a friendly chime. A smiling Claudia Benson opened the door. She was slim, about five-foot-four, with short salt-and-pepper hair. She was wearing a blue floral-patterned dress. He guessed her age to be early-sixties. She invited him to come into the living room. The inside of the house smelled of something mouth-watering baking in the oven.

He removed his hat. "I'm sorry for your loss, ma'am."

"Oh, thank you, Deputy Rivera, but I filed for divorce and changed my name back to Benson a couple of years ago." She gestured toward a stuffed chair. "Please have a seat." Rivera settled into the comfort of the chair. She moved to a love seat directly across from him and sat down, smoothing her dress over her knees. "I'm sorry Feb got himself into trouble but as far as I'm concerned, it was over between us years ago."

"You two weren't getting along?" Rivera opened his notepad and extracted a ballpoint pen from his shirt pocket.

She shook her head. "When he first came to Moab about ten years ago, I fell for him. He was interesting, fun, and attentive. After my first husband died, I figured I'd never marry again. Which was fine. I was fifty-one years old and had a lot of interests and activities. My daughter lives in Moab with her husband and their children, so I spent a lot of time with the grandkids. I was happy.

"Then Feb came into my life and sort of swept me off my feet. He was a real charmer. I guess I felt like a young girl again. I thought about him all day long and looked forward to the times we would spend together. He thought we should get married and was persistent about it. Finally I gave in. It was fun for a few years, but one day his personality abruptly changed. He became preoccupied and distant. He'd been a social drinker since the day I met him. Charming and entertaining. But then he started drinking way too much. I couldn't handle it and when I'd say something to him about it, he'd become even more distant. It was like I was living with a stranger. Eventually I realized I wanted my old life back."

"You said he became preoccupied. Do you know what was on his mind?"

"He never told me. I tried to get him to talk but he would always shut me out. When he wasn't at one of his bars, he spent a lot of time alone in the office in the back of the house. I have no idea what he was working on back there. He wouldn't tell me. Anyway, over the years, I got fed up with him." She looked past Rivera, as if reflecting. Then she shrugged. "Maybe he got fed up with me, too. When he disappeared three years ago, I assumed he just took off and went back to New York. And I was glad he was gone."

"Did you report his disappearance to the police?"

"I mentioned it to the Moab Chief of Police, but I didn't make a formal report. I was relieved the whole thing was over."

"When was the last time you saw him?"

"I remember the exact date. My birthday is October fifteenth. He disappeared two days earlier, three years ago."

An overweight tabby cat sauntered into the room. It paused for a moment and looked up at Rivera.

Considered him. Then it walked over to the love seat, jumped up, and settled into its owner's lap. Claudia Benson began rubbing it behind the ears. Rivera could hear the purring from where he was sitting.

"Did he have any enemies that you know of?"

She thought for a moment. "No, actually everyone liked him. He was quite popular around town. He was always interested in people, what was happening in their lives, and how they were doing. He had a knack for getting people to talk about themselves. He remembered everything about them. And people loved his storytelling. He had a great imagination. I could never tell which of his stories were true and which were exaggerations, but they were always entertaining." She hesitated, her eyes now moist. "Most of his stories were about things that happened in New York City. He was an investigative journalist for the *New York Times* for a while, maybe ten years. Then he free-lanced for about fifteen years. I think he must have been very good at what he did."

"Why did he leave New York and move to Moab?"

"He told me that one day he just decided he'd had enough of the big-city grind. His friend Sam Enderle had retired as a sportswriter from the *Times* and moved to Grand Junction. It was Sam who talked him into moving out west. But instead of Colorado, Feb came here. He said it was the rugged beauty of the red rock canyons that made him choose Moab. And he wanted to experience living in a small town. It was different in so many ways from what he was used to. He liked to point out that New York City had eight-million residents to Moab's six-thousand."

"Do you have a photograph of February I could borrow?"

"No, I don't. I threw them all away after he disappeared." Her expression hadn't changed but her voice now had an edge to it. "His face was the last thing I wanted to see."

Rivera changed the subject. "What did he do with his time when he wasn't working in the office or out at a bar?"

"There was a serious side to him. He seemed to have developed a strong interest in local government. When we were first married, he asked me a lot of questions about how things worked in a small town. He wanted to learn everything he could about the city government, the county government, the budgeting process, and things like that. He attended most of the open council meetings and asked lots of questions. I guess it was the journalist in him. He couldn't change his spots. But mostly, he drank and worked in the back office."

"What did you do with the things in his office after he disappeared?"

"Nothing. I just closed the door and left everything as it was. It's a small room and I didn't need the space.

I guess in the back of my mind I expected him to come back one day and collect his belongings."

"So the office has been untouched all this time?"

"Yes. Well, no. Not exactly. A couple of days after he disappeared, someone broke into the office. Probably some kids. There's an outside door from the office to the backyard. It was seldom locked. A couple of the drawers in the filing cabinets were open. So was the desk drawer. The only thing I noticed missing was the computer box under the desk. I don't know what to call it. It was part of the computer, about the size of a wastepaper basket." She looked at Rivera, her eyes asking for help.

"I know what you mean. It's called the hard drive."

"Thanks. I'm so bad with technical things." She managed a self-deprecating laugh. "Anyway, the computer was old so I wasn't particularly concerned about it. But after the theft, I locked the back door."

"Did you report it to the police?"

"No. The computer was probably not worth much. I didn't see any point in filling out all that paperwork."

Rivera heard a ding. The cat jumped out of Claudia's lap as she stood up with a smile. "Excuse me for a moment. The cookies are done and I need to get them out of the oven right away so they don't overcook. They're for my grandson's birthday party tonight." She smiled proudly. "He's six."

"Do you mind if I look around the office while you're in the kitchen?"

"Not at all. Go right ahead."

Rivera slipped on a pair of latex gloves, entered the small office, and scanned it. The far wall contained an exit door and a pair of windows facing the backyard. Against the left wall was a desk with a padded swivel chair. A Dell computer monitor and printer were sitting atop the desk, along with a telephone, some newspapers, a stapler, and a beer mug containing an assortment of pens and pencils. A long narrow shelf above the desk was filled with Indian pots, shaman figures, and inexpensive Navajo-made kachinas. On his right were two grey filing cabinets and a small table with a stack of magazines and newspapers. The room had a musty smell and the newspapers had yellowed with age. On the wall over the filing cabinets was a framed Tom Till print of Mesa Arch. A layer of dust had settled on everything.

Rivera noticed the missing hard drive immediately. The connecting cables were lying on the floor under the desk. He wondered if the unit had in fact been stolen by kids as Claudia thought, or if it was taken by someone who feared it might contain incriminating information. The open drawers of the desk and filing cabinets certainly suggested the room had been searched.

He rummaged through the newspapers on the desk and the table. They were mostly old copies of the weekly Moab *Times-Independent* and a few copies of the *San Juan Record*, the weekly newspaper that served San Juan County to the south. The desk drawer contained a Frontier telephone book for southeast Utah, a box of staples, a strip of postage stamps, and a scattering of rulers, pens, and business cards. The business cards were all for local merchants.

He pulled open the drawers of the file cabinets, one at a time. Each of the eight drawers contained manila folders filled with old copies of New York City newspapers and national magazines. He scanned a few of the publications. Each contained an article with the byline *February Flanagan*. The newspapers included the *Tribune*, the *Times*, the *Post,* and the *Daily News.* Among the national magazines were *The New Yorker*, *Atlantic Monthly*, and *Harpers*. The files were arranged in chronological order starting in the year 1975 and continuing through 2000.

Rivera massaged the back of his neck as he reflected on the collection of Flanagan's life's work. It must have been the thing he was most proud of. And now the pages were yellowed and hidden away in dust-covered filing cabinets. The sum-total of a career forgotten by all but a few.

He closed the office door behind him and removed the latex gloves. In the kitchen, Claudia was using a spatula to transfer the cookies from cookie sheets onto plates. He thanked her for her cooperation, asked her not to disturb anything in the office, and told her a technician would come over later this afternoon to dust the room for fingerprints. She looked startled. "Just routine," he assured her. He started toward the front door.

"Just a minute, Deputy Rivera. These are for you." She handed him a brown paper bag warm to the touch. "They're oatmeal-raisin cookies. I hope you like them."

He smiled. "They're my favorite."

As he left the house and walked back to his pickup, he wondered just what kind of project Flanagan had been working on behind closed doors. He also wondered what became of the hard drive.

4

BEHIND WENDELL COSGROVE'S HOUSE was a detached two-car garage which served as the artist's studio. Both the house and garage were painted the grey-green color of sagebrush with dark green trim. Rivera walked up the driveway and around an old Volkswagen van to the garage. The side door was open. He knocked and stuck his head inside.

Cosgrove looked up from the oil painting on his easel and smiled. "Hi, Manny. Come on in." Cosgrove was a tall lanky man with a long grey ponytail, a three-day stubble, and an easy smile. "How's everything going?"

"Fine, Wendell, thanks." Rivera walked over to get a closer look at the painting, a mesa landscape of golden grasses punctuated with dark green junipers. A morning fog was lifting and rays of sunshine were slanting through. "That's a beautiful painting."

"Thanks. It's a scene I remember from a hike up on Cedar Mesa a couple of years ago." He pointed with his brush toward a well-worn stuffed chair in the center of the room. "Have a seat, Manny."

Rivera lowered himself into the chair and took a quick survey of the studio. On the far wall hung three of Wendell's completed paintings: a red rock canyon landscape, a scene depicting Delicate Arch in the moonlight, and a waterscape showing a group of rafters fighting their way through white-water rapids. Cosgrove had an uncanny way of using shadows to make his paintings look three-dimensional. Which explained why his work was so popular. He was also a part-time sculptor. On a workbench in front of the window was an assortment of the artist's bronze shaman sculptures.

"I need to talk to you about February Flanagan."

Cosgrove's expression changed from relaxed to troubled. He slowly shook his head. "Terrible shame about Feb. It'll be a long time before I get over it. He was a damn good friend."

"You knew him better than anyone in town. Can you think of a reason why anyone would have wanted to kill him?"

Cosgrove dipped his brush into a small can of turpentine and wiped it off with a rag. "No, I can't. Feb was an interesting, intelligent, fun-loving man who loved life. I have no idea why anyone would have wanted to harm him, much less kill him."

Rivera nodded. "His wife told me he had an interest in local politics and business dealings. Did he ever talk about that?"

Cosgrove managed a smile. "All the time. Feb was an investigative journalist at heart. He was retired but his instincts weren't. I had the impression he was highly regarded in New York journalism circles. I suppose he couldn't shut off his naturally suspicious side when he retired in Moab. He saw conspiracies and crooked dealings everywhere he looked."

Rivera took out his notepad and clicked open his pen. "Could you give me an example?"

"Sure. Feb was real interested in BLM land transactions. You're aware that sometimes the BLM engages in land swaps with private individuals and corporations. The government might need more land in a particular area to preserve habitat or build a logging road or whatever. So they'll swap land they own that has commercial value for the land they want. Feb was convinced some of the deals were crooked, with the BLM getting the short end of the financial stick, and some government official getting a large payoff in the process."

"I've heard that theory before. But no one's ever produced any evidence. Any other examples?"

"Well, let's see. He often questioned the zoning decisions out in Spanish Valley. Said some of the County Commissioners were real estate developers who would benefit from zoning changes. I told him I thought he was wrong. I know all the commissioners. They're honest people. And the zoning decisions seemed appropriate for an expanding community. But that didn't deter Feb."

Rivera waved away a fly circling his head. "What else was he interested in?"

"He used to talk about the Department of Energy project for moving that giant plateau of uranium mill tailings from alongside the Colorado River up to the Crescent Junction area. He thought the whole thing was a waste of money. He said the radioactive dust emitted into the air by moving the pile was more of an environmental hazard than the threat of a flood washing the stuff into the river. He also thought the real motivation for moving the tailings was that some influential political donor wanted to develop a riverside resort on the property after the tailings had been cleared."

Cosgrove continued on, citing other examples of Flanagan's suspicion of evil doings in local politics. Then he summed up his thoughts. "I'm not really sure Feb believed these theories himself. But he liked to talk about them as though they were highly plausible. Maybe he was just trying to be entertaining. He loved to raise people's eyebrows."

"None of that seems like the kind of thing that would get a man killed."

Cosgrove nodded in agreement. "Yeah, it's all pretty standard Moab gossip."

Rivera sat there for a moment, thinking. "Do you happen to have a photograph of him?"

"Sure. Be right back."

Cosgrove left the studio and went to his house. Rivera waited, studying Cosgrove's artwork and wondering if he himself had any artistic talent. He recalled a few feeble attempts when he was an adolescent: playing the clarinet, oil painting, making pottery. All were total failures, motivated solely by the desire to meet girls. He decided he probably wasn't cut out for artistic endeavors. His cell phone buzzed. He unclipped it from his belt and pressed the answer button. All he heard was a hissing sound, reminding him once again that he'd forgotten to replace the failing battery. One more item for the to-do list.

Cosgrove returned to the studio and handed Rivera two photographs. One showed Flanagan standing in front of a bar with a big smile on his face. Behind the bar were shelves filled with assorted liquor bottles. In one hand, he was holding a glass filled with an amber liquid and some ice cubes. His other hand was extended, palm up. He looked as though he had just finished telling a funny story and was enjoying his audience's reaction. The other photograph showed him sitting in a room Rivera recognized as his home office, feet propped up on his desk, looking over his shoulder at the camera with a contagious grin. His face was long and narrow with smile lines extending outward from his eyes. His full head of wavy hair was a mixture of brown and grey. He was barefoot, wearing faded jeans and a yellow T-shirt.

"Thanks for these, Wendell. And thanks for your time."

"One other thing, Manny. I always had the feeling that Feb was working on something else, something he never talked about, not even to me. I don't know exactly why I thought that. Just an odd sense that something unspoken was going on in my friend's life."

When Rivera returned to his office, he found Dr. Pudge Devlin sitting there, waiting for him. The pot-bellied florid-faced Devlin was one of his favorite people. He was formerly a successful surgeon in Denver, but one day, realizing he wasn't enjoying life, he sold his practice and moved to the Moab area. Now he was a part-time Medical Examiner and a full-time vintner. Devlin's small vineyard in Castle Valley produced a good Merlot which was highly sought after by the Moab locals. However, it was always in short supply as Devlin consumed most of it himself. With typical Devlin humor, he'd explained to Rivera one time that the only reason he drank so much of it was to reduce the supply and thereby keep the price high.

Devlin was usually upbeat with a mischievous smile on his face and a twinkle in his eye. Today his expression seemed serious and grim.

"Manny, I've completed the February Flanagan autopsy. I'll get my formal report over to you later, but I wanted to give you a quick heads-up on what I found. The slug to the back of his head was the cause of death. And my initial estimate of the date of death was about right. Three years give or take a month." Devlin hesitated, cleared his throat. "But that's not all, Manny. It looks like Flanagan was made to suffer a great deal before he was killed."

"What do you mean?"

"I mean he was badly beaten before he was shot. Six ribs were broken, four on one side and two on the other. His left forearm was broken in two places. He also had a dislocated shoulder and a broken clavicle. Several of his front teeth were missing."

Rivera stared at Devlin and slowly shook his head. Said nothing.

Devlin continued. "The killer not only wanted Flanagan dead, he wanted him to suffer before he died. He must've been very unhappy with Flanagan. Or crazy." He stood up to leave.

"Thanks, Pudge," said Rivera tentatively.

Devlin started toward the door, then stopped and looked back. "Be careful with this one, Manny. You're looking for a real nasty character."

5

TUESDAY MORNING PROMISED ANOTHER beautiful day in Moab. The sky was a deep blue and the temperature was in the low sixties and rising. After breakfast at the Rim Rock Diner, Rivera sat in his office sipping coffee and staring at the wall. The things he'd learned from Devlin yesterday had been disturbing to say the least. What kind of person would give a sixty-three-year old man a severe beating and then kill him? And why?

Last evening, when he'd briefed Sheriff Bradshaw on the case, they'd agreed it would be a good idea to keep confidential the gory details of Flanagan's beating. No sense spooking the tourists. Later, after he'd gone home, Rivera tried to make some sense of the whole business. He'd searched his mind for a plausible motive but found none. There was nothing going on locally that added up to such a vicious killing. Moab was a quiet, friendly, fun town where people came to enjoy themselves. No one he'd ever met here, whether visitor or resident, seemed capable of such an act. Flanagan must have been poking into something that angered someone intensely. Someone who turned out to be a monster. Last night while trying to fall asleep, it was all Rivera could think about.

This morning he had a different problem. He was trying to force his mind to focus on the Flanagan case. But images of Vivian Ramos kept intruding on his thoughts and distracting him. Finally he decided to quit fighting it. He let his thoughts take him back to the Maze Overlook and the weekend they'd spent there. Hiking and exploring by day and cuddling in front of the campfire by night. She'd told him she liked spending time with him, thought he was very intelligent, and loved talking with him. She also said she liked his wavy brown hair, his smile, and his muscular arms and shoulders. She always knew just what to say.

He was eager to see her again soon but the Chief of Nursing at the Moab Regional Hospital had assigned her as lead nurse for the Surgical and Emergency Services Unit on the night shift this week. So Rivera would just have to wait. Fortunately they had a date for Saturday night. Four more days. He planned to take her to the Sunset Grill for wine and a candlelight dinner. He'd reserved a table next to the window so they could watch the sunset from high atop the east bluff overlooking Moab. After that they would take a moonlight drive through Arches National Park. Then …. A voice snapped him out of his reverie.

"Manny, you have a visitor."

It was Meredith, the new receptionist. She was just out of high school, but at five-foot-eleven was already as tall as Rivera. Being slender and wearing a short skirt made her seem even taller.

"Hi, Meredith. Who is it?"

She read from a business card. "His name is Reynolds. William Vanderberg Reynolds, the Third." She put a sarcastic emphasis on *The Third* and smiled, exposing a set of upper and lower braces. "It says here he's a freelance journalist from *New York City*." More emphasis. She rolled her eyes, handed the card to Rivera, and left.

Rivera grinned broadly as he rose from his chair. Meredith was young but already possessed a well-developed knack for sizing up people. He walked out to the waiting area. There was a man perched on the edge of a chair wearing pressed grey slacks, a flowery lavender shirt, and black loafers with tassels. His left wrist sported a flashy gold watch. Medium height and medium build, he had shiny black hair neatly parted on one side. He looked to be in his late-forties. He definitely wouldn't be mistaken for a local, Rivera thought as he approached him.

"Mr. Reynolds, I'm Deputy Sheriff Manny Rivera. Can I help you?"

"Good morning, Deputy. William Reynolds from New York City." He extended his hand and clicked on a perfunctory smile.

Rivera shook the man's hand, noticing he had unusually white teeth.

The smile clicked off. "I understand you're in charge of the February Flanagan murder investigation," he said.

"Yes, that's correct."

Smile clicked on. "I think I might be of some help. I was good friends with Feb back in New York. In fact, he was my mentor. We worked on many cases together and he taught me most of what I know about investigative journalism. No one wants to see his killer brought to justice more than I do. I thought I could be of assistance by providing you with some background information on Feb."

"Well, thank you." For an instant, Rivera wondered why Reynolds hadn't just telephoned him and saved the long trip. "That's very much appreciated. Let's go to my office and talk. Can I offer you some coffee?"

"That would be fine."

Rivera got the man settled in one of his visitor's chairs and started the conversation with small talk.

"First time in Moab?"

"Yes. Very different from what I'm used to. Not many trees out here."

"No. Our large trees grow mostly in the mountains where there's a reliable supply of rainwater. Aspens, spruce, so forth. The mesa tops have smaller trees. Pinyon pine, scrub oak, juniper. There's less rain at the lower altitudes, so down here it's mostly brush land with a little juniper."

"I saw some of those junipers on the drive down here from Salt Lake City. They look more like bushes than trees."

Rivera laughed. "A friend of mine went back east to Hartford on business a few years ago. He told me the trees there were tall and dense. The horizon was so close it made him feel claustrophobic. He said in Connecticut, people thought the trees *were* the view. Out here, he said, trees like that would just *block* the view. I guess it's just a question of one's perspective."

"I suppose so. It just seems so barren and empty around here. And the quiet would drive me crazy."

Rivera found himself feeling sorry for the man and at the same time being slightly irritated by him. He'd noticed years ago that there were generally two kinds of people in the world. One talks about the things they like in life, the other tells you the things they don't like. Rivera preferred the former. And this guy was definitely the latter. It was time for a change of subject.

"How did you happen to hear about Flanagan's death?"

"An associate of mine who works for the *New York Times* picked up the story on one of the wire services. He remembered that Feb and I worked together back in the eighties and nineties, so he called me." Reynolds took a sip of coffee from his mug. He pursed his lips and blinked rapidly as though his culinary standards had just been egregiously violated. He set the mug down and slid it aside. "The print journalism community was surprised when Feb retired and moved to Utah. I guess he just wanted to get out of the rat race. I heard he married a local."

"Yeah, Claudia Benson. But they weren't getting along. She filed for divorce after he disappeared."

"Did she have any idea why Feb was killed?"

Rivera shook his head. "Not a one."

"I can't imagine anyone in Moab wanting to kill Feb. It doesn't look like there's much going on around here. But he had plenty of enemies in New York."

"Enemies?" Rivera's interest in what the man had to say clicked up a notch.

"Sure. He exposed a lot of corruption and illegal activity back there. Government, unions, contractors, the mob, sports, you name it. He'd received several death threats over the years. I suppose someone from New York could have come out here and killed him. You know, maybe a guy gets out of jail after serving his time and comes here looking for Feb. Even though

Feb was retired and out of the game, revenge is still a possible motive. Do you have any leads?"

"No. We're just getting started."

"What have you got so far?"

Rivera was beginning to get the feeling he was giving out more information than he was getting back. "I interviewed a couple of his friends for routine background information. As I said, we're just getting under way. Could you fill me in on Flanagan's activities back in New York?"

"Oh yes, of course." The smile reappeared but was quickly replaced with an earnest expression. "Well, first of all, Feb was well-known as a hard-nosed investigative journalist. The best in the business. During the first part of his career, he worked for the *New York Times*. Later he freelanced for various New York City newspapers and national magazines. Eventually they were all trying to outbid each other for his stories."

"How did he operate?"

"Whenever he got a hunch or a tip about some activity involving abuse of public funds or malfeasance in office, he pursued it like a bloodhound. He spent a lot of time researching public records in the courthouses, digging through newspaper archives, and interviewing working-level employees. He was smart and his instincts were good, so he could usually tell when he was on the trail of something significant. He would organize his facts, postulate theories about what was going on, and then put pressure on lower level bureaucrats for more information by threatening to expose them in some way. Then he worked his way up the organization until he had the whole story. After that, he would enlist the help of a friend in the Attorney General's office and a couple of New York City Police Department investigators he knew he could trust. He was the driving force on several high-profile investigations that led to busting some important and powerful people. And of course, exclusive stories would appear in the newspapers under his byline."

"Could you give me some examples of the cases he broke?"

"Sure. The first case I remember started with a tip from a building contractor who had unsuccessfully bid on a job to construct a community of public-housing apartments in the South Bronx. He'd been underbid by sixteen percent. The project was won by a company who had an unusually high success rate with its bids for city contracts." Reynolds delivered his oratory with a staccato pacing, his eyes darting from place to place as he spoke. "The unsuccessful bidder periodically examined the construction site as the apartments were being built. He wanted to learn how the winner was able to do the job for so much less than he could. His motive was simply to educate himself, but it was soon obvious to him that the materials being used didn't meet code. And eventually he discovered that the plumbers and electricians on the project weren't licensed. Feb got wind of all this from the unsuccessful bidder and went to work."

"What year was that?" asked Rivera.

"I believe it was 1985. Anyway, Feb traced the problem to a group of city building inspectors who were accepting bribes from the contractor. The inspectors involved had wealth beyond their station in life. Feb was finally able to crack the case by identifying the city inspectors whose wealth was modest. He presumed these were the honest ones. After interviewing several of them, he found one that was willing to talk. Off the record, of course. From this one man, Feb learned how it was done. The inspectors were chosen and the bribes paid even before the job was put out for bids. The crooked bidders knew in advance they could cut costs on materials and labor and get away with it. As a result, they were able to low-ball their bids. It didn't take Feb long to learn which inspectors were on the take. There was a correlation between the contractors who routinely won projects and the inspectors assigned to those jobs. And Feb didn't stop there. He realized that those higher up in the organization had to be involved. Someone had to assign the right inspectors to the right jobs. Of course, the higher-ups would also be receiving a piece of the action. It took Feb nearly a year, but he eventually learned the corruption went all the way to the top of the City Building Inspection Department. When the dust finally settled, twelve people had been sentenced to prison."

Rivera's pen moved quickly as he jotted down extensive notes. He found himself becoming fascinated with February Flanagan.

Reynolds continued. "I wasn't involved in that case but it brought Feb onto my radar screen. I decided I wanted to work with him and learn from him. So one day I visited him and offered my services as an understudy and assistant. After that, we were pretty much a team."

"What else did Flanagan work on?"

"In the early nineties, we learned about slush funds that were routinely assigned to each of the city council members. There was nothing wrong with that per se. The money was a standard part of the city budget. The funds were intended to help not-for-profit organizations in each council member's district. The money was doled out at the council member's discretion. We did a routine check on the organizations receiving funds to determine which community activities were being supported. It turned out that one organization receiving a substantial amount of money each year was run by family members of the councilman doling out those funds. When we asked to inspect their books, they granted us permission. Unfortunately, that night there was a fire. All the records were lost and the computer system was destroyed."

"So you hit a dead end?"

"The arson was pretty brazen. But, no, that didn't stop us. We talked to their computer systems guy, a volunteer who worked on weekends. He told us he was worried about the old computer system they were using. It turned out he'd been using his home computer for weekly backups just in case. We turned everything over to the Attorney General's office and broke the case the next day."

Rivera now took a greater interest in the contents of the file cabinets in Flanagan's office. His curiosity had risen to the point where he wanted to read through some of the articles Flanagan had written.

"Flanagan sounds like a Woodward and Bernstein kind of journalist. You must have learned a lot from him."

"I did. But I carried my weight, too." Reynolds seemed annoyed. "We worked as a team."

"Any other cases you can tell me about?"

"Sure. In 1996, we stumbled onto something big at the Brooklyn Marine Terminal. It's a small containerized shipping port with docks, warehouses, and trucking terminals. Over the years, the Russian Mafia had infiltrated the facility's management and the Longshoreman's Union there. They'd set up a big-time smuggling and hijacking operation. Huge quantities of cocaine, heroin, and marijuana arrived weekly. The stuff was hidden inside shipping containers that contained legitimate merchandise. Federal inspectors on the take let the stuff pass through. But that's not all. Containers with expensive imports like flat-screen TVs were stolen simply by being loaded onto a Mafia truck instead of the correct truck. The entire operation was corrupt. I called Feb's attention to a missing person report when I learned the missing man was an inspector at the marine terminal. From there, we took it on as a team. The inspector was never found. We presumed he was somewhere at the bottom of the East River. We worked on the case for over a year. The net result of our investigation was an FBI bust of the whole operation and the dismantling of that branch of the Russian Mafia. Most of them ended up in prison serving long sentences."

Rivera continued taking notes. "Please go on," he said, wanting to hear more.

For the next hour, Reynolds recounted numerous tales of the Flanagan/Reynolds team and their exploits in New York. The stories included bid rigging in bridge inspection contracts, payoffs in the granting of liquor licenses, high-class prostitution involving prominent clients, fixing of sporting events, murder for hire, and out-and-out theft of city funds. It was an eye-opening treatise on what goes on in a big city. Reynolds finished by saying, "The spirit of Boss Tweed lives on."

Rivera wasn't sure what that meant. He guessed it had something to do with New York City corruption but didn't want to ask. He put his pen back in his shirt pocket, thanked Reynolds for the information, and asked how long he'd be in town.

"As long as it takes. I plan to do some investigating of my own. I won't rest until Feb's killer is found and punished." Reynolds stood up to leave. In what seemed to be an afterthought, he added, "If I find out anything important, of course I'll let you know about it."

Rivera watched Reynolds depart. He had an uncomfortable feeling about the man's presence in Moab.

6

RIVERA REFLECTED ON HIS MEETING with William Reynolds as he gulped down the last of his coffee. Basically, he didn't care for the man. Or trust him. He reeked of deception. And the idea of Reynolds conducting his own investigation didn't sit well with Rivera. Of course, there was nothing he could do about it as long as Reynolds didn't interfere with his own investigation. And who knows, maybe he would actually come up with some useful information.

Rivera reached into his in-basket and pulled out the report on the fingerprint dusting in Flanagan's office. The only prints found belonged to Claudia Benson and February Flanagan himself. The technician's report said he secured Flanagan's prints from a pair of sunglasses and a plastic ruler in the desk drawer. He'd taken Claudia's prints directly from her and reported that she'd giggled throughout the entire process. She couldn't wait to tell her grandchildren about it. The one interesting fact was that no prints had been found on the hard-drive cable connectors. There should have been thumb prints on them. Clearly the connectors were wiped clean. Someone had stolen the hard drive and it wasn't kids.

Rivera leaned back in his chair, hoisted his feet onto his desk, and looked out the window at the LaSal Mountains. The aspens had begun turning gold, a result of the cold nights at the higher altitudes. He reviewed what he had so far. It amounted to nothing more than tales of Flanagan's New York investigations, reports of his opinions on local government projects, and the items in the evidence locker. There wasn't much to go on. His general hypothesis was that Flanagan had been working on a secret project, that someone had found out and felt threatened, and that Flanagan had been killed because of it. The theft of the hard drive made the theory all but certain.

An image of the evidence locker contents kept reappearing in Rivera's mind. He wasn't sure why but he had a vague sense that he'd missed something that was staring him in the face. He'd learned early in life from his grandfather not to ignore this kind of mental nagging. The elderly wise man had told him it was usually the subconscious mind trying to call something important to the attention of the conscious mind.

He returned to the evidence locker and emptied Flanagan's box onto a table. He sorted the contents and stared at them, studying one item, then the next, forcing himself to concentrate. Finally it hit him. It was the key ring. There were three keys on it. One was a Schlage, most likely the house key. The other two were General Motors keys. Flanagan had had a vehicle.

He drove back to Claudia Benson's residence and rang the doorbell. She opened the door and smiled. "Welcome back, Deputy Rivera. Did you come back for some more of my oatmeal-raisin cookies?" She laughed, apparently enjoying her own humor.

He laughed too. "That's not why I came, but if you're offering more of those delicious cookies, I'm definitely accepting. That first batch you gave me is long gone."

"Well, come on in and I'll get you another bagful. Your friend, Mr. Reynolds was here before lunch. He likes oatmeal-raisin cookies too."

Rivera followed her into the kitchen. "Reynolds? What did he want?"

"He wanted to talk to me about Feb. He said they had worked together back in New York. He told me about a lot of investigations they'd conducted as a team. He wanted to know all about Feb's life in Moab, what he did, who his friends were. He seemed like a nice man so I answered his questions." She paused. "Funny, though, I don't recall Feb ever mentioning his name. Anyway, he showed me pictures of some men and asked if I'd ever seen any of them in Moab. I looked through them but I didn't recognize a single face." She walked over to the countertop and began tugging on the lid of a cookie tin. "Did you want to ask me some more questions about Feb?"

Rivera wondered why Reynolds hadn't shown the pictures to him. "Just one question. Did Feb own a vehicle?"

She looked up at Rivera, as if a sudden realization had just occurred to her. "Why, yes, he did. I completely forgot about it. It's an old Chevrolet automobile. It's out in the garage behind the house. I never go in there anymore. It's full of spider webs and dust."

"I'd like to take a look at it."

"Sure, go right ahead. The garage door isn't locked. Just pull up on the handle."

Rivera walked up the driveway to the garage. A pair of western bluebirds flew from their perch on the rooftop, squawking at the interruption. He grasped the handle on the garage door and raised it up. Sheets of red rock dust fell as the door rose. Rivera turned away, blinking.

After the air cleared, he peered into the garage. Claudia was right. The inside was a jungle of cobwebs. He grabbed an old broom. With long sweeping motions, he cleared the webs away from the car. The vehicle was a white 1992 Chevrolet Lumina. It was covered with a layer of red-rock dust and all four tires were flat. He opened the driver's side door and slid in. The interior was relatively clean. In the glove box was the usual complement of ownership and inspection papers, maps, repair receipts, and tire warranties. Also a half-empty pint bottle of Jim Beam. He looked under the floor mats, above the sun visors, and in the back seat. Nothing helpful. Then he pulled a lever and slid the front seat all the way back. He peered underneath it. He found a comb, some candy wrappers, several pieces of pop corn, and a dime.

He got out and walked to the rear of the car. He extracted Flanagan's key ring from his pocket, unlocked the trunk lid, and raised it. Besides the spare tire and tire-changing tools, the trunk appeared empty. He noticed the far corner of the black mat on the trunk's floor was pushed up slightly. He pulled it forward and discovered a cardboard accordion-type portfolio stashed underneath. He removed it and walked out of the garage into the light.

Inside the portfolio were five manila file folders. He scanned the handwritten titles on the folder tabs:

Insurance Fraud
Wedding Article
Bus Accident 1968
Utah Department of Health, Moab Office
Illegal Immigration

Rivera considered the titles. None of them seemed to resonate with the topics mentioned by Cosgrove as being of interest to Flanagan: zoning changes, BLM land sales, mill tailings, and so forth. These subjects were entirely different. Maybe the files pertained to local investigations Flanagan had been conducting in secret.

As he drove back to the office, Rivera hoped that one of the files contained information that would lead to the motive for Flanagan's murder.

7

RIVERA REMOVED THE FIVE FOLDERS from Flanagan's portfolio and spread them out across his desk.

His curiosity caused him to start with the file entitled *Insurance Fraud*. What in the world did insurance fraud have to do with Moab? The two seemed incongruous. He picked up the file and flipped it open. Inside were copies of four articles printed from various insurance information websites. He scanned them. They summarized the common forms of insurance fraud, claims made to insurance companies to collect money under false pretenses. Health care fraud typically involved claims made by health care providers for work not actually performed. Life insurance fraud consisted of claims submitted for insured people who had not actually died. Automobile insurance fraud often took the form of "arranged" accidents to collect insurance money for back and neck injuries. Staged accidents on municipal property were discussed. So was arson. One article stated the insurance industry lost thirty billion dollars each year due to fraud. It was all pretty dry reading.

Rivera reached into the brown paper bag Claudia Benson had given him and extracted a cookie. He slowly chewed it and washed it down with coffee. He failed to see what insurance fraud had to do with anything local. He closed the file and set it aside.

He opened the file marked *Utah Department of Health, Moab Office*. It contained an organization chart for the Moab satellite office of the Utah Department of Health, a list of duties for that office, and a photo of the staff at their annual picnic. The photo had been clipped out of the *Times-Independent*, Moab's weekly newspaper. The organization chart was dated 2005. Linda Anderson was the Director back then and still was today.

The third file was entitled *Bus Accident 1968*. It contained several old newspaper clippings from the *Times-Independent* and the *Salt Lake Tribune*. The articles described a gruesome accident. A school bus containing eleven children from a small orphanage in Thompson Springs had careened off a bluff in the Book Cliffs area. The driver, the orphanage director, and all eleven children had been killed. They were on their way to visit the Range Creek Ranch on a school project. The kids' ages ranged from six to nine. The file also contained two color photographs. One picture showed the front of a large two-story house with the doors and windows boarded up. He turned the photo over. A handwritten caption read *County Orphanage at Thompson Springs*. Rivera was vaguely familiar with the old orphanage. It had closed years ago. In fact, most of the town was now defunct, except for a few businesses that survived by catering to visitors exploring the rock art sites in Sego Canyon. The other photograph showed a grouping of eleven small gravestones. The caption on the back read *Thompson Springs Cemetery*.

The *Wedding Article* file contained a *Times-Independent* story about a wedding which took place in 2005. The article was accompanied by a picture of the happy couple posing with their best man and maid-of-honor. The groom was a high-profile real-estate developer in Moab named Skip Kennison. Rivera recognized the name immediately.

The fifth file was entitled *Illegal Immigrants*. It contained seven articles on illegal immigration downloaded from various political and news websites. The articles focused on some of the more creative methods employed by aliens to gain entry into the U.S. and blend unnoticed into society.

Rivera sat back in his chair, absentmindedly reached for another cookie, and bit off a piece. Flanagan had been looking into these five topics and he'd kept his interest in them secret from everyone, even his wife and closest friend. The old journalist was becoming more and more intriguing.

The phone rang. It was Wendell Cosgrove.

"Manny, I just had a visit from a guy named Williams Reynolds from New York. He was here asking me the same kinds of questions about Flanagan that you were asking. He said he was helping you with the investigation. I didn't see any harm in talking to him, so I answered his questions. He showed me a couple of dozen pictures of various men. I think the pictures were photocopied from newspapers. He asked if I'd ever seen any of them around Moab. Some looked like businessmen or politicians, some looked like hoods. Anyway, I didn't recognize any of the faces. Just thought you should know."

After he hung up the phone, Rivera's knee-jerk reaction was to get a little steamed about Reynolds. First of all, he hadn't shown Rivera the photos or even mentioned them. And secondly, he was in no way assisting in the investigation. He was misrepresenting his role. Rivera inhaled a deep breath and let it out. He sat back and allowed the logic of the situation to calm him down. Reynolds had no knowledge of the files February Flanagan had kept in the trunk of his car. Reynolds would always be on the wrong track, chasing after the stories Feb had been telling in the bars. So there was really nothing to be concerned about. Nevertheless, it was beginning to feel like a competition.

He finished off the last cookie in the bag, brushed the crumbs off his shirt, and left the building. He hopped into his pickup and drove to the Moab satellite office of the Utah Department of Health. It was located in a one-story white building next to Moab's three-screen movie theatre. He entered and walked down the hallway to the Director's office. Linda Anderson was sitting behind her desk, her face buried in a thick computer printout. She was a small athletic-looking woman in her mid-fifties with weathered skin and short auburn hair. He tapped on the door jamb of her office. She looked up and smiled.

"Hi, Manny. C'mon in and have a seat." She took off her glasses and laid them down on the printout.

"Good morning, Linda." He sat down, noticing the framed photographs of border collies on her wall and desk. She was a well-known dog breeder, highly respected throughout Utah and Colorado. "I know you're busy so I won't take a lot of your time. I'm investigating the February Flanagan murder and I'd like to ask you a few questions."

"Sure."

"I found a file folder of his that contained an organization chart for this office dated 2005. There was also a listing of the Health Department's areas of responsibility and a newspaper article with a photo from the office picnic. Did you know Flanagan?"

Her smile broadened. "Oh, yes. Feb was in here often, asking questions about everything we did. I was never sure what he was up to, but his visits were always a fun occasion. He seemed to focus on a different subject with each visit, always probing into some aspect of our charter. I felt like he was putting us under a microscope, trying to see something that no one else had seen. But his visits were enjoyable, even though I always had a sense he was trying to catch us doing something dark and evil." She let out a squeaky laugh.

"Do you remember what he was particularly interested in?"

"Anything and everything. This department has many roles. Our responsibilities include clinical health services, immunizations, environmental health, birth and death certificates, communicable disease prevention, cancer screening, and so forth. We have a broad health charter and focus primarily on special-needs families. We're overseen by a nine-member Board of Health. Feb asked about all of our activities at one time or another."

"Does any one area stand out in your mind?"

"No, not really. I'd say he was in here a dozen times, maybe more. Each visit focused on a different subject. And he usually pursued it in depth, wanting to understand all the facets and nuances. He was a very intelligent man and had a knack for asking really insightful questions."

"OK, thanks, Linda. If you think of anything else about his visits, let me know. I'm trying to narrow down his interests, trying to find a motive for his murder. Unfortunately, it seems like he was interested in everything."

"I'll think about it some more and call you if I come up with anything."

Rivera returned to his office. Not knowing which file to focus on, he was beginning to feel a bit frustrated. If he tried to head out in five different directions at the same time, he wouldn't make much progress with any of them. He needed some help. He picked up the phone and dialed Chris Carey's number. Carey was a friend and a retired newspaper journalist who had worked for several Utah newspapers over the years including the Moab *Times-Independent*. He'd helped Rivera on a few previous cases.

"Chris, It's Manny. Have you got any free time these days?"

"You bet I do, Manny. How can I help?" There was anticipation in his voice.

Rivera knew Carey was more than a little bored in retirement and was always interested in taking on new projects. Rivera confidentially filled him in on the Flanagan case, telling him everything he knew except the brutality that preceded Flanagan's death. He asked if Carey could dig into the newspaper archives and pick up where Flanagan left off on the 1968 bus accident and the Moab wedding. Specifically, Rivera wanted to know if there was any hint of wrongdoing or scandal related to either of these events. If there was not, then

Rivera could eliminate two of the five files as possibilities and focus on the remaining three.

"I'll start right away, Manny."

Rivera thanked Carey and hung up the phone just as Meredith walked into the office and handed him a file. It contained Flanagan's credit reports and telephone records. Flanagan hadn't used the credit card at all during the twelve months preceding his death. And the debit card was used solely to make cash withdrawals from his checking account. Never for purchases. Usually two-hundred dollars was withdrawn twice a week. He seemed to operate exclusively on a cash basis. There were automatic deposits into his checking account from three mutual fund companies each month. It looked to Rivera like Flanagan had been in pretty good shape financially. The telephone records showed nothing unusual. Mostly local calls to private residences and Moab merchants.

Around six o'clock that evening, Rivera left the office and headed home in his pickup. The LaSal Mountains to the east were glowing a pink-orange color as the setting sun dropped behind the Moab Rim. On Main Street, the town was coming to life. Tourists were returning from the backcountry in their Jeeps and filling up the restaurants and bars. Nearly everyone was wearing a T-shirt and either shorts or jeans.

As he drove past Pasta Jay's restaurant, he noticed a familiar face sitting alone at one of the tables on the outdoor patio. He pulled his unit over to the curb, got out, and walked back to the restaurant.

As Rivera approached his table, William Reynolds looked up and produced one of his mechanical smiles.

"Good evening, Deputy Rivera. Won't you join me?" He gestured toward a chair.

"No thanks, I'm on my way home. I noticed you sitting here and decided to stop by and see how your investigation is coming along."

"No meaningful progress yet. How about you?"

Rivera ignored the question. "I understand you've been showing some pictures around town. What's that all about?"

Reynolds hesitated a beat. "They're people from New York that might have had an interest in killing Feb. People who either lost their jobs or went to jail because of one of his investigations. The photographs were in the newspapers. You remember, the revenge theory I suggested."

"I remember. I'll need to get copies of those photographs. You neglected to mention them to me."

Reynolds produced a tentative smile, his face slightly flushed. "Oh, sure. No problem. But I don't have them with me. They're back at the motel. I'll bring them to your office tomorrow morning so you can make copies."

8

RIVERA TURNED INTO THE GRAVEL DRIVEWAY of the two-bedroom house he rented near the center of town. He grabbed his briefcase, slid out of his vehicle, and ambled up the walkway toward the front door. Just as he reached it, he heard the telephone inside start ringing. He fumbled for his keys, unlocked the door, ran to his bedroom, and grabbed the phone on the fourth ring.

"Hello?"

"Manny, it's Chris Carey. I've done some preliminary work on the two stories you asked me to investigate."

"Great, Chris. What did you find out?"

"First of all, let's talk about the bus accident. The *Salt Lake Tribune* had a fairly complete description of what happened. The Thompson Springs Orphanage had nineteen residents, ages one to nine. The director's name was Eileen Brewster.

"The older kids from the orphanage, ages six and above, were on a field trip with Brewster to the Range Creek Ranch up in the Book Cliffs area. They were traveling in the orphanage bus, driven by a man named Curtis Timmons. A tour had been arranged with the ranch owner to show the kids some ancient-Indian arti-facts and dwellings. That valley has lots of petroglyphs and pictographs inscribed on the canyon walls.

"The road from Highway 6 to the ranch goes up a steep incline with lots of tight switchbacks and then down the other side into the narrow valley where the ranch is located. It's a rough unpaved road with loose gravel and stones. The police report said the bus got too close to the edge of the road and the weight of the bus caused the ground to give way. The theory was that heavy rains earlier in the week had softened the shoulder. The bus slid sideways off the road, rolled fifty feet down a steep embankment to the edge of a cliff where it plunged three hundred feet into a rocky wash. Brewster, Timmons, and all eleven kids were killed. The names of the orphans were withheld from the article. They're all buried in the old Thompson Springs Cemetery."

"How awful. Was there any sign of criminal behavior? Any reason for February Flanagan to initiate an investigation?"

"Brewster had an assistant named Theodora Sanders. I managed to track her down. She's now living in Provo. She had stayed back at the orphanage with the kids who were too young to go on the trip. I called her and quizzed her about the whole affair. The only thing she could add to the story was that Timmons, the driver, was a recovering alcoholic. She had talked to him on the morning of the trip just before the bus left. She said he was quite sober and had been for two years. Beyond what was in the article, that's everything I've been able to find out so far."

"Sounds like there's no reason to believe a crime was committed. Maybe Flanagan was interested in the accident from a human-interest point of view. What about the article on the wedding?"

"A marriage took place in June of 2005 between Kay Lord, age thirty-six, and Byron "Skip" Kennison, age forty-three. She's a history teacher at the high school and he's a very successful real estate developer. You've seen his office on Main Street. They live in town and also own ten acres out in Castle Valley. I understand they plan to build a home out there some day. He recently developed a residential subdivision called MountainView in San Juan County just across the county line. The lots are selling well and a few homes have been built. Some people characterize Skip as ambitious but to me he seems like a good man who's become successful by working hard.

"The picture that accompanies the article shows the bride and groom flanked by Meriwether Williams, the best man, and his wife Claire who was the maid-of-honor. Meriwether and Claire got married in Salt Lake City a few months later. He's forty-eight and manages a company called Seven Star Investments. You've probably seen him around town. He has a beard and walks with a cane. He was broadsided some years ago by a teenage drunk driver in Colorado. The accident left him crippled. She's thirty-eight and the daughter of a former Utah state senator. Meriwether is an elder in his church and she's active in several charitable activities in town. They're both highly respected citizens and seem to be happily married. Despite his bum leg, he won the kayak race down the Colorado River three years running. As I understand it, his investment company is closed to outsiders and handles primarily the Williams's own money and that of some of his wife's relatives. His office is in the Uranium Building."

"I don't know any of them personally," Rivera said. "But they all have fine reputations around town. Any idea why Flanagan would have had an interest in them?"

"None at all, but I'll keep digging."

"Okay, thanks, Chris."

After their conversation, Rivera went to the kitchen and turned on the radio. It was perpetually tuned to KCYN, "Moab's Canyon Country Radio," transmitting from high in the LaSal Mountains. The Highwaymen were singing *The Last Cowboy Song*. He placed a frozen sausage pizza in the oven, set the temperature according to the instructions on the box, and opened a cold Budweiser beer. After a couple of refreshing swigs, he walked over to the ten-gallon aquarium on his kitchen countertop. Its occupants, twenty-odd multi-colored guppies, darted toward him in anticipation of a meal. He dropped in a pinch of tropical fish food and began reflecting on the Flanagan case as he watched them eat.

It seemed clear that Flanagan had enemies from his days in New York. No doubt about it. It was possible Reynolds was right, that someone from New York who had a score to settle with Flanagan had located him in Moab and gotten even. If that were the case, whoever had killed him was now long gone. He was probably back in New York where he was no further threat to the residents of Grand County and where no deputy sheriff from Utah would ever find him. The case would likely end up unsolved. That scenario couldn't be ruled out but was it likely? Rivera had a hard time accepting the timing. A revenge killing seven years after Flanagan left New York just didn't seem probable. The files in the trunk of Flanagan's car hinted at a more likely circumstance. Flanagan was working on five local investigations, serious investigations that he shared with no one, and one of these had gotten him killed three years ago. But the revenge theory proposed by Reynolds still lurked as a possibility.

After finishing the pizza and starting on a second can of beer, Rivera moved into the living room. His original plan for the evening was to kick back and watch a movie. Millie Ives, the sheriff's dispatcher, had loaned him a DVD which she said was her all-time favorite movie. He read the case cover. It was Robert Redford's *Milagro Beanfield War*. Rivera wanted to relax and enjoy the movie, but he couldn't get his mind off the Flanagan case. Instead, he decided to study the materials related to the case once again, hoping for some new insight or inspiration.

He emptied his briefcase on the kitchen table and reread the case file, the contents of February's five files, and the interview notes he'd jotted in his notepad. The only thing that resonated as a new possibility was something Claudia Benson had said. She'd mentioned a friend of Flanagan's from New York, someone who had worked with him at the *New York Times*. He flipped back through the pages of his notepad and found the name. Sam Enderle, now living in Grand Junction. Grand Junction was just across the Utah-Colorado border, a little over an hour's drive from Moab. He called Enderle and scheduled a visit for the following day at ten in the morning.

As Rivera slid February's files back into the accordion portfolio, light from the ceiling fixture reflected off something white in the bottom of the portfolio. He reached in and pulled out a business card which he hadn't noticed before. The name on the card was Frank McKelvey of the McKelvey Investigative Service in New York City. Rivera wasn't sure if the card had fallen out of one of the files or had been placed separately in the portfolio. No matter. He would call McKelvey in the morning to see what else he could learn about the mysterious February Flanagan.

9

BART WINSLOW SAT AT the Formica table in the kitchenette of his small cabin, eating a bowl of granola, planning the day ahead. As soon as he finished breakfast, he would make an important telephone call to New Jersey, a call that hopefully would result in a lot of cash for Bart. Then he would leave for his job as systems analyst in the Moab office of the Utah Department of Health. He looked around at his humble surroundings. The tiny A-frame had been built with spruce logs by his father over thirty years ago. It sat behind his parents' home in Moab at the back of their half-acre lot. There was a single living area, a kitchenette to the rear, and a loft with a double bed upstairs. He loved his parents and thoroughly enjoyed spending time with them. He particularly liked hiking the backcountry with his father, a former outfitter and guide who knew the surrounding canyons, mountains, and rivers better than anyone in the county. Ever since his older brother had been killed, Bart and his father had become much closer. He liked that.

But he really had a burning desire for a place of his own. It wasn't just that he wanted more space and better things. He felt embarrassed that, at age twenty-nine, he was still living at home. He was sure that was why girls seemed to have little interest in him. Every day on his way to work, he drove past the new community of southwestern-style condominiums under construction. Many had sold but there were still several available. He pictured himself living in one of them with a brand-new vehicle parked in the driveway. The image that always came to his mind was a pretty girl with long dark hair sitting on his back patio sharing a bottle of wine with him and watching the sunset. But he couldn't afford the down payment on a condo, much less the price of a new vehicle. His job as the Health Department's computer guru just didn't pay a whole lot.

His desire to own a condo inevitably led him to consider looking for a better position. He knew he could earn a lot more money if he was willing to leave Moab and move to a large city where his computer talents would be in high demand. He was a self-taught computer scientist who barely finished high school, but he had a knack for understanding the inner workings of computers. Based on his demonstrated capabilities, most high-tech companies would hire him for three times his current salary. But he couldn't bear the thought of leaving the land of red rock canyons and the weekend hikes with his father to out-of-the-way, seldom-seen places.

He sipped on a glass of orange juice and stared out the window at the leaves of a cottonwood tree shimmering in the morning breeze. He reflected on his technical expertise and how it had grown over the years. He'd become curious about computers early in life. Not the usual game playing that most kids do. He'd started doing that when he was four. By age nine, he'd outgrown games and become intensely interested in how computers work. On various internet sites, he'd diligently studied computer architectures until he understood how program instructions move, modify, and store data. In his mind's eye, he could see digital numbers flying through adders, accumulators, and inverters, shuttling into and out of registers, and being stored in and retrieved from memory locations. It made so much sense to him. He could do binary arithmetic in his head by age ten. By twelve, he was writing code using the C language and the UNIX operating system. He'd mastered most aspects of software engineering by age fifteen. His specialty was data communications security, and its kissing cousin, computer hacking. The work he performed at the Health Department wasn't particularly challenging. In fact, it was downright boring. But it provided an excellent cover for his side business.

He picked up his cell phone, pressed a couple of buttons, and speed-dialed a number in Newark.

"Ralph, it's me, Bart. Did you close the deal with our new client?"

"It's done as of an hour ago, cousin. They need to buy two new identities and they need them in a hurry."

"Two? I thought we were talking about just one."

"Nope, they want two."

"This is going to take longer than I thought."

"We don't have a lot of time. They need them right away. They're being hunted by the Feds and need to change their identities quickly. Don't you have a couple of names from that bus accident you can use?"

"We've already sold ten of them. There's only one left unused."

"We split ten thousand dollars for each identity, cousin. If you want your half, you'd better come up with another name fast."

"Male or female?"

"Both male. Both look in their late forties, early fifties. They're from Chicago."

"What professional background do they want?"

"One should be an accountant, the other an engineer."

"Type of engineer?"

"Mechanical."

"Okay. I'll get back to you later today." Bart paused. "By the way, Ralph, we should raise our prices. I don't think we're charging enough. And I need some serious money for a down payment on a condo."

"Let me think about that." He clicked off.

Bart sat back and considered the new project. The basic idea was to identify a deceased individual with a birth certificate on file who would have been about the right age had he or she lived. Then remove all traces of the individual's death record, both locally and at the state level. Add a college degree and a job history and you've created an instant new identity with a legitimate birth certificate on file. A very marketable item.

He and Ralph had done this ten times over the past seven years. It all started about a year after Bart was employed as a systems analyst in the Moab office of the Utah Department of Health. One day, there was a sudden need for an experienced systems analyst to fill in for an ill employee at the State Health Department's Office of Vital Statistics in Salt Lake City. Bart spent four weeks there managing the main computer system and developing new software as needed. During that time, he envisioned the possibility of creating authentic new identities and selling them. Thinking he might never again have a chance to program the Salt Lake City computer, he wrote and installed a covert program which would allow him to penetrate the computer's security firewall and access its operating system from the terminal in his Moab office. It was unlikely anyone would ever detect this tiny alteration to the system's software. It was only two-hundred lines of code nestled within three million. Nevertheless, it would allow him easy access to the state's super-secure computer system for the purpose of modifying death records in the database.

When he explained to his cousin the idea of creating and selling new identities, Ralph jumped at the chance and they became partners. Bart took care of the computer end of the operation and Ralph, whose circle of friends wouldn't make anyone's social register, did the marketing. It had worked well but they'd only made one or two sales each year. Bart wanted a more aggressive marketing program. He would bring up the matter with his cousin again soon.

He walked over to his small roll-top desk, turned on his laptop, and hit a few keystrokes. A list of names from the bus accident of 1968 appeared. Eleven deceased orphans. The only unused name from the tragedy was Anthony L. Chester, born September 7, 1962. That would do for one of the new identities. He would have to do some research to come up with a second usable name.

The bus accident information had been a goldmine for him. Eleven names of deceased people no one would ever check on. Bart had deleted their death records, both locally and at the state level. They had died in 1968, long before death records had been computerized in Utah. Because of his job, Bart was a vital statistics specialist and knew not only the ins and outs of birth and death certificate processing, but also the history of the Utah system. In the old days, paper death certificates were filled out by the mortuary director and the attending physician and then submitted to the registrar at the local office of the State Health Department. The registrar approved the certificate, kept a copy in the local office, and forwarded the original to the Office of Vital Statistics in Salt Lake City. That's all there was to it. It was a simple and effective system but advances in technology made change inevitable.

Some years ago, the process had been computerized. The new system was called EDEN, an acronym for Electronic Death Entry Network. Now, new death certificates were prepared on-line. A blank electronic Certificate of Death was accessed from the Office of Vital Statistics. The attending doctor, the mortuary director, and the local registrar, using their individual authentication passwords, filled out their portion of the form via encrypted communications links. When completed, the form was stored electronically in the computer's database in Salt Lake City. An electronic copy was also retained in the local district office. There was no longer any paper to handle.

After the computerized process was put into service, it was a secure and convenient way to handle new deaths, but there was still the question of what to do with all the old paper death certificates. A decision was made by the State of Utah that the paper certificates would also be computerized. One by one they were scanned, and a photographic image of each was stored in the computer. Accessing a particular death certificate image was done by locating the individual's name in a master directory. That would, in turn, connect the correct death certificate image. When the scanning project was completed and the original paper certificates no longer needed, they were boxed up and placed in cold storage. There was rarely a reason to consult them again.

The process Bart had followed with the eleven orphans was straightforward. As systems analyst for the local office in Moab, he was able to delete their names from the local death records in the Moab computer system without difficulty. And it was a simple matter for him to remove the paper death certificate copies in the local file cabinets and destroy them. Which he did. But the records which existed in electronic form at the Office of Vital Statistics in Salt Lake City also needed to be deleted. The covert program he had installed while working there allowed him to do just that.

The secure link between his terminal at the Moab office and the main system at the Office of Vital Records allowed him to request that a blank Certificate of Death form be displayed on his terminal. If he typed the nonsense letters XyZvW in the deceased's zip code block on the form, it would trigger the covert program and he would penetrate the system's firewall, gaining access to its operating system. Once through the firewall, he could make alterations to the death record database.

It was impractical to change or remove computerized death certificates because the older ones, the ones of interest to Bart, had been scanned and were therefore stored as visual images. Changing them pixel-by-pixel would be too tedious a task. Instead, he simply altered the master directory, substituting a made-up name for the deceased person's name. As a result, the death certificate image was still in the computer system but there was no way an operator could access it. It was virtually non-existent. He had done this for the death records of all eleven orphans. There was nothing he could do about the original paper death certificates filed in cold storage in Salt Lake City. He would just have to trust they would remain boxed up, collecting dust.

Anthony L. Chester would serve as one of the new identities. Bart would figure out later how to develop the second identity.

He spoke into the intercom connected to his father's office in the main house.

"Morning, Dad. Are you in the office?"

"I am, son. Are you leaving for work?"

"I'm just about to go. Are we on for a hike this weekend?"

"We sure are. I'm looking at topo maps of the area around Hanksville right now. I'm thinking we should hike down into Robbers Roost Canyon, Butch Cassidy's old hideaway. Maybe we can find some traces of Butch and his Wild Bunch gang. It's more than a weekend hike, though. Could you get a couple of extra days off, maybe make it a four-day hike?"

"Sure. I've got lots of vacation time accrued. And things have been kind of slow at the office. I'll ask Linda today if I can take off Monday and Tuesday."

"Great. I'll plan the trip. By the way, your mother is going to City Market today. She wants to know if you'd like pork chops for dinner."

"Sounds great. See you tonight."

The old pickup coughed on Bart's first attempt to start it, reminding him he desperately needed a new vehicle. The engine caught on the second try. He thought about two things as he drove to work. The first was how lucky he was to have his mother's cooking every night and a father who was his best friend. The second was how badly he needed to increase his income. He and Ralph would have to raise prices. Maybe double or even triple them. And Ralph would have to hustle a lot more business.

10

MANNY RIVERA LOVED BREAKFAST. Getting up early and heading for the Rim Rock Diner to meet his buddy Emmett Mitchell for sausage, eggs, hash browns, wheat toast, and coffee was a favorite part of his day. The place was like a second home to him. It was an old diner, reminiscent of the fifties, with vinyl-padded booths seating four and a U-shaped counter with swivel seats. Framed black-and-white photographs of early twentieth-century Moab filled the walls, giving testament to the city's history as an old mining town. The diner was frequented by locals and generally the same people showed up each morning. Most of the waitresses had worked there for years and knew the customers on a first-name basis.

He parked his pickup in the parking lot next to the café and walked to the front door. He pulled it open and was greeted by the familiar smells of breakfast and the sounds of people enjoying each other's company. He spotted Butch, the short-order cook and waved to him. Butch, a rotund man with a perpetually sunburned face, was wearing a white paper hat. He smiled and waved at Rivera with a large spoon. As Rivera headed toward his usual table in the far corner, he passed by the "old-timers booth," normally occupied by four grizzled men in their eighties discussing the good old days when Moab was a thriving mining town and they were young men prospecting for uranium. But this morning there were only three of them sitting there. Rivera stopped at their booth.

"Howdy, fellas. Where's Freddie this morning?"

Jimmy Jensen, the self-appointed spokesman for the group, laughed heartily through a full reddish-grey beard. A large man, he was hard of hearing and spoke in a loud voice. "Why, Freddie's out staking a claim. I guess he got excited after all our talk last week about the world running out of oil and the price of uranium going through the roof. He told me that after thinking about it, he figured that most of the country's electricity will come from nuclear power plants in the future. Damn fool's out there on that BLM land south of Mineral Canyon staking out a claim as we speak. Says he's sure there's uranium ore in that Chinle layer a couple of hundred feet below the surface. Says he can smell it." He laughed again, louder this time, slapping his large hand on the tabletop. "That area was prospected over and over back in the fifties. There's nothing out there."

Willie Wilson, one of Jensen's companions who had been listening attentively, quietly slipped out of the booth and headed purposefully for the door.

"Hey, Willie, where are you going?" shouted Jensen.

Willie glanced back without stopping. "Could be Freddie's on to somethin'."

Jensen and his other companion, Stanley, looked wide-eyed at each other for a long moment, then nodded and slid out of their seats. "Hey, Willie, wait for us," Jensen called out, as they lumbered toward the door.

Rivera was still chuckling as he arrived at his booth and sat down. The old prospectors still had uranium fever.

Rivera loved this town and everyone in it. He felt lucky to be living here. He missed his extended family in Las Cruces, but this is where he wanted to be. He looked out the window and saw Emmett Mitchell parking his San Juan County Sheriff's Department pickup, just as Betty arrived at his side. She poured him a mug of coffee. Betty, a waitress at the diner for fifteen years, was in her fifties and had four or five ex-husbands. Her bleached-blonde hair was piled haphazardly on her head, and the top three buttons of her too-tight white uniform were open. She was smiling and chewing gum.

"Mornin' handsome," she said in a sultry tone. "Heard you have a girlfriend."

Rivera looked at her and smiled. This was the start of her daily flirtation with him. "Good morning, Betty."

"If things don't work out with her, you know where to find me."

Rivera had no comeback for that. And he didn't want to say anything that would encourage her.

She stared at him, grinning and slowly chewing her gum, apparently waiting for a response.

As Rivera desperately searched his mind for a way to change the subject, Mitchell arrived at the booth and sat down. Just in time.

Betty poured him a mug of coffee. "You hunks want the usual?"

They nodded and she left to deliver the order to Butch.

During breakfast, Rivera briefed Mitchell on the details of the Flanagan case. He always appreciated the opportunity to discuss his cases with his friend as Mitchell was fifteen years older and had a lot more experience in law enforcement. He was a deputy sheriff in San Juan County, the county just south of Grand County.

"So it comes down to this," Rivera concluded. "Did someone from New York with a revenge motive come out here and kill Flanagan or did Flanagan's investigations in Moab get him too close to something, something so important that it was worth killing for?"

Mitchell shrugged and finished his coffee. "Could have been either. It's too soon to tell. Keep digging, Manny."

Rivera stopped by his office to take care of a couple of things before making the drive to Grand Junction to visit Sam Enderle. First, he placed a call to the McKelvey Investigative Service in New York City. A pleasant female voice announced, "We're not here right now. Please leave a message and we'll call you back as soon as we can." So he did. He explained that he was a deputy sheriff from Grand County, Utah, and that February Flanagan's decomposed body had been found last Saturday. He stated that Flanagan had been shot in the head and buried under a remote stone ledge behind a pile of rocks three years ago. He added that McKelvey's business card had been found among Flanagan's things. Rivera requested a call-back and left the numbers for his cell, office, and home phones.

The second thing he did was to tell Meredith that Mr. Reynolds from New York City would be arriving this morning with a sheaf of photographs and that she was to make a copy of each and leave them on his desk. "And try to behave," he added with a grin.

She smiled and curtsied. "Of course, Deputy Rivera."

After driving directly into the sun for nearly an hour, Rivera was relieved to arrive at the Enderle residence. It was a tan stucco home with terra-cotta roof tiles located in a cul-de-sac. The front yard consisted of crushed red-rock and was populated with high-desert plants and cacti. He removed his sunglasses, walked to the front door, and rang the doorbell.

Mrs. Enderle, a tall slender woman with curly grey hair, answered the door.

"Come in Deputy Rivera. We've been expecting you," she said in a pleasant voice.

She showed him into the living room and invited him to sit on the couch. She offered him a cup of coffee which he gladly accepted. "Sam's on the phone. He'll be along in just a minute," she said, then excused herself and went to the kitchen.

Rivera looked around the room. It had a cozy feel to it. It was filled with early-American furniture covered with plaid upholstery and smelled of potpourri. Framed photographs of children and teenagers were everywhere. He noticed a photograph of a smiling Rudy Giuliani with his arm around a man sitting in a wheelchair. They were both wearing New York Yankees caps. The photo was autographed but Rivera couldn't read the inscription from where he was sitting.

Mrs. Enderle returned with a cup of coffee and placed it on the table in front of Rivera.

"Thanks very much," he said. He took his first sip just as Sam Enderle rolled into the living room in a wheelchair. He introduced himself, shook hands with Rivera, and positioned the wheelchair directly in front of him. Enderle was an older man, late-seventies, Rivera judged. He had a long face and a few remaining wisps of white hair on his head. He wore thick rimless glasses which made his eyes appear unusually large and inquisitive. After the polite preliminaries, Rivera took out his notepad and began asking questions.

"Mr. Enderle, how long did you know February Flanagan?"

"We met in nineteen-eighty, I think it was. At the *New York Times*. He worked for the City Editor and I worked for the Sports Editor. We hit it off right away, became good friends."

"Can you tell me about him, what kind of man he was, what he worked on, and how he conducted his investigations?"

Enderle sat back and smiled. "I sure can."

11

TRAFFIC WAS LIGHT ON Interstate 70 as Rivera headed west back toward Utah. He steadily increased his speed until he reached seventy-five miles-per-hour, then clicked on the cruise control and slid his foot off the accelerator. He settled into his seat for the drive home.

As he came up over a rise and crossed the state line, a mass of darkness to the south caught his eye. A tall anvil-shaped cumulo-nimbus cloud, bright-white on top and black underneath, was moving across the LaSal Mountains on spindly feet of lightning. Rain clouds were always a welcome sight in the high desert. Even if the rains never arrived where they were needed, dark thunderstorms rumbling across the distant landscape always made for a beautiful sight.

Rivera reflected on his two-hour discussion with Enderle as he passed a caravan of eighteen-wheelers. He began sorting out what he had learned about Flanagan.

First, he was a top-notch investigative journalist with three Pulitzer Prizes to his credit. He was one of the best in the business. Enderle confirmed the things Rivera had been told by others.

Second, Flanagan held his cards close to the vest. He never discussed what he was working on, not even with Sam. The only exception had been one time when they'd worked together on a case involving the fixing of basketball games at a local university.

Third, Flanagan operated like a wanted man, a paranoid wanted man. He knew certain people were out to get him. He had no home, preferring to stay in hotels. He changed his residence often, occasionally as much as two or three times a week. He kept very little in the way of files. Nothing in the office, and very little in his possession. He had a good memory for details and was careful to destroy notes when they were no longer needed. He used public telephones for business and operated on a cash basis to avoid leaving a paper trail.

Fourth, he had developed an interesting way of interviewing public servants. He would ask detailed questions about many different aspects of their work. Only one of those aspects would be the subject of his investigation. But the interviewee never knew which one. It never stood out from the others.

Fifth, Flanagan couldn't stand William Reynolds. Reynolds was a wealthy, spoiled, incompetent weasel. He was always trying to find out what Feb was working on and publish it under his own byline before Feb could break the story. Feb had no respect for him.

And sixth, corruption had ruined Flanagan's family life when he was fourteen. He'd grown up in the Bronx as the only child of Irish-Catholic lower middle-class parents who worked hard to give him a good education. At the age of fifty-four, his father had lost his job as supervisor of a bridge inspection and maintenance crew. The company he worked for replaced him with the inexperienced son of a city councilman. The councilman was very influential in awarding contracts to the firm and pressured the owner into hiring his son "in a suitable supervisory position." After that, Flanagan's father couldn't find a job and turned to drinking. One night, in a drunken stupor, he staggered in front of a delivery truck and was killed. Flanagan's mother went into a deep depression. Flanagan did his best to support her by working for the *New York Tribune*, first in the circulation department and later for the city editor. Sadly, she died of pneumonia two years later. Flanagan joined the Army and served six years in an intelligence unit as an analyst. He left the Army and put himself through New York University using the G.I. Bill, earning a degree in journalism. Flanagan hated corruption and dedicated his life to exposing it.

Rivera had asked Enderle if he had any theories about why Reynolds would have come all the way to Moab to investigate Flanagan's killing.

"It's simple," Enderle had replied. "Reynolds wants to write an article or more likely a book on how he solved the murder of his friend and mentor, while recounting all the fine work they did as a 'team' in New York City."

At Mile Marker 190 on the Interstate, the green exit sign for Thompson Springs caught Rivera's eye. He looked at his watch. He had plenty of time to detour into the mostly-abandoned town and spend a few minutes looking around. He was particularly interested in seeing the cemetery where the kids from the 1968 bus accident were buried. He was also curious about the old orphanage. He drove down the exit ramp and headed into town.

There wasn't much left of Thompson Springs. Once, before the mines closed, it was a thriving area which supported a small community of hard-working citizens. Some of the homes were still occupied and a few businesses seemed to be hanging on, but most of the buildings were boarded up or falling down. Up ahead on the left he saw rows of grey and white gravestones in a field of golden grasses. He turned onto the gravel lane that led into the cemetery and parked. He stepped out of his vehicle and stretched his back. It was a warm day with the temperature in the low eighties. The sky was bright blue and criss-crossed with white vapor trails left by high-altitude jet aircraft. The only sounds to be heard were the dull hum of the distant traffic on the interstate and the chirping of unseen birds in the trees and bushes.

Rivera shaded his eyes and scanned the cemetery. It was surprisingly well manicured. It didn't have the disheveled look one would expect of an abandoned cemetery. Then he saw the reason why. An old man wearing bib overalls and a straw hat was hoeing weeds from one of the gravesites. His skin was badly weathered from the sun and he looked to be well over eighty years old. Rivera approached him.

"Howdy," said Rivera.

The man looked up, adjusted his bifocals, and squinted at Rivera.

"Howdy." He studied Rivera's uniform. "We don't get many visitors from the sheriff's office out this way." The man got straight to the point.

"My name's Manny Rivera. I'm investigating the murder of a man named Flanagan whose body was found a few days ago near Labyrinth Canyon."

"This here's a long way from Labyrinth Canyon. You sure you're in the right place?"

Rivera nodded. "Yes sir, I'm sure." This was followed by a long silence. The old fellow wasn't making things any easier. He just stood there, leaning on his rake, staring at Rivera.

Rivera attempted to break the ice, bring the conversation to a more cordial level. "I was interested in taking a look around the cemetery. See who's buried here."

"Only dead people, far as I know."

Now it was Rivera's turn to stare silently at the old man. Seconds passed like minutes.

A smile slowly appeared on the man's face. He laughed and extended his hand. "My name's Steve. I was just having a little fun. Don't see many folks out here anymore. How can I help you?"

Rivera smiled, breathed easier, and shook the man's hand. He had a surprisingly strong grip, despite the arthritis which had severely gnarled his fingers.

Rivera glanced over Steve's shoulder and scanned the graveyard. "The cemetery looks beautiful. Are you the caretaker here?"

"Not officially. I like to stay busy and working here as a volunteer gives me something productive to do with my time. Gives me a purpose. And besides, all my friends are buried here. They deserve to have the place looking nice." He took out a red and white handkerchief and wiped his forehead. "I spent my whole life here in Thompson Springs. I used to oversee this place, back when the town was alive and this was still an operating cemetery. That was my office over there." He pointed to a small building constructed of cut grey stones with a peaked slate roof. "I was in charge of burials, sales, record keeping, maintenance, you name it. I retired fifteen years ago. Now I'm just a maintenance man."

Rivera nodded. "I'm interested in learning more about eleven children who were killed in a school bus accident back in 1968. I understand they're buried here."

"Yes, they are. I remember the day we got the news. Everyone around here was in shock. Those kids were like the community's own children. The town was in mourning for years." He pointed with his free hand. "They're buried over there in the northwest corner of the cemetery."

"Thanks. I think I'll go have a look." Rivera started to walk off.

"I'll go along and show you where they are. It'll save you some searching."

Rivera walked slowly so Steve, who was hobbling along using the rake as a walking stick, could keep up. Neither man spoke, as though they were part of a solemn procession. As they neared the site, a ground squirrel stood up on his haunches, peered at them for a long moment, then scampered off to its burrow. Next to a Russian olive tree, Rivera saw eleven small gravestones cut from what appeared to be light-grey shale. Each gravestone had a first name and last name chiseled into its face along with a birth date and a date of death. The gravestones were rough-hewn and unpolished, and the engraved characters were uneven. The markers were obviously made by a non-professional volunteer. The horror of the bus accident was underscored by the identical date of death on each stone: *May 26, 1968.*

Rivera took out his notepad and jotted down the names and dates from the gravestones.

"The accident knocked the wind out of our little town," said Steve. "Broke its spirit. Eventually the remaining kids were shipped off to foster homes and the orphanage was closed down and boarded up. It stood there vacant, a constant reminder of what had happened. Ollie Anderson threatened to burn it down. Said the sight of it depressed everyone in town. But he never did." He paused, shook his head. "If those kids had lived, they'd be in their late forties, early fifties by now. And maybe the community wouldn't have died."

The two men slowly returned to Rivera's pickup.

"Where's the old orphanage building?" asked Rivera. "I'd like to take a look at it."

"Go back to the pavement and turn left. It's about three blocks, on your right."

"Many thanks, Steve."

Rivera pulled up to the curb in front of the orphanage and stepped out of his vehicle. The building was an expansive two-story wooden structure. The doors and windows were covered with planks. Much of the paint had peeled off the white clapboards and the brick steps leading up to the front door had partially collapsed. The yard was overgrown with weeds and the picket fence across the front yard had fallen and rotted. There wasn't a whole lot to see. As he turned to leave, a breeze kicked up and he heard a groan. He looked back. It was the old windmill on the side of the building. Two of its vanes were missing and three others were bent. Yet it slowly rotated, grudgingly responding to the breeze, still trying to do its job, struggling to remain relevant. In a way, it reminded him of Steve. And that made him think about his own life. What would he be doing when he was Steve's age? What would his life be like? Eventually that led him to more pleasant thoughts involving Vivian.

Rivera followed I-70 west to the Crescent Junction exit and turned south on U.S. 191 heading back toward Moab. He was thinking about his visit with Sam Enderle and the things he'd learned about February Flanagan. Flanagan had been scrupulous about keeping his investigations to himself. Maybe even fanatical. The hotel hopping would get old for most people after a few days. But Flanagan had done it for years. No wonder he'd wanted to retire and move west. The things Enderle had told him fit the pattern of Flanagan's behavior in Moab. The secrecy, the deceptive questioning, the minimal paper trail, it was all the same. And Reynolds had totally misrepresented his relationship with Flanagan.

Rivera turned his thoughts to the specifics of Flanagan's murder. He was badly beaten before he was killed. So where did the beating take place? Was he beaten, then transported to Labyrinth Canyon and executed there? Or beaten and shot, then the body transported? Or had everything taken place out by the canyon? Rivera was familiar with only a small segment of Labyrinth Canyon. He wasn't acquainted with the section where Flanagan's body had been found. He'd studied the photographs in the case file but they weren't sufficient to give him a feel for what might have happened out there. Maybe visiting the site would trigger some useful lines of thought. He decided to spend what was left of the day driving the back roads that led to the bluff overlooking Labyrinth Canyon to see the place for himself.

12

RIVERA APPLIED THE BRAKES, slowed his pickup to twenty miles per hour, and turned right on Route 313. He followed the pavement through Sevenmile Canyon, then drove up the switchbacks to the top of the mesa. He continued until he reached the Dubinky Well Road cutoff. There he turned right onto the gravel and pulled his vehicle to a stop. From the case file, he extracted the quadrangle map showing the location of the crime scene and studied it, planning his route across the backcountry to Labyrinth Canyon. One wrong turn and he'd miss the burial site by a mile. He proceeded a short distance to Spring Canyon Road, then turned left and followed it for six miles into a remote vastness of rocky canyons, arroyos, and brush. Just before reaching a large Navajo sandstone outcropping, he located a two-track primitive road heading southwest and slowly followed it five miles through open country as its quality steadily degraded, finally becoming a series of potholes, ruts, and steps.

The track ended at the edge of a bluff where Hell Roaring Canyon fed into Labyrinth Canyon. Hell Roaring Canyon was currently dry, but a heavy rainstorm in the right place could abruptly change all that. Thus the name. Rivera stepped out of his vehicle and scanned the horizon. The sun was low in the sky and clouds were gathering to the west beyond the Henry Mountains, promising an eye-catching sunset.

The temperature had begun to drop and a slight breeze now rustled the brush. The tan-grey Book Cliffs were visible to the north and the LaSal Mountains dominated the eastern horizon. The rays of the setting sun struck the flank of the thunderstorm passing over the LaSals, creating a complete double rainbow. What a beautiful spot to set up camp. Maybe he could come back here with Vivian some day. He walked over to the edge of the bluff and peered into Labyrinth Canyon and the Green River flowing some eight-hundred feet below. A rubber raft with four lounging occupants looked tiny as it silently drifted downriver.

Dusk was approaching and Rivera knew he would be losing light fast. It was time to quit admiring the scenery and get to work. After studying the hand-drawn map in the case file, he headed north across the cap rock, sidestepping clumps of blackbrush, Mormon tea, stunted junipers, and boulders. After some searching, he found the yellow crime-scene tape which outlined the stony grave that had concealed Flanagan's body for three years. Rivera lowered himself onto a nearby rock and sat there, trying to picture what might have happened.

Stan, the Moab Tavern bartender, had said Flanagan walked between his home and the bar rather than driving since he lived only three blocks away. Perhaps the killer had abducted Flanagan late one night while he was walking home from the bar, a bit tipsy or worse. The assailant might have knocked Flanagan unconscious, loaded him into a vehicle, and driven him out of town to this remote place. The vehicle must have been high-clearance and four-wheel-drive. The site was on a peninsula of mesa bordered on the north by Spring Canyon and the south by Hell Roaring Canyon. Both were deep chasms which fed into Labyrinth Canyon. There was no road by which a vehicle could access the site except the one Rivera had driven in on, and it definitely required a backcountry suspension and drive train.

Flanagan probably had remained unconscious during the drive, since there was no sign he'd been bound. No rope, no tape. The killer might have finished the beating at the end of the road, shot Flanagan there, and carried the body to this place. Flanagan weighed about one-hundred and seventy pounds, so the killer had to be strong. Rivera studied the rocks which had been used to hide the body. Most were small, but some looked like they weighed forty or more pounds. They had to have been gathered down by the edge of the bluff where loose rocks were available, then carried up the incline to this spot. The killer was definitely male and strong.

Other than the killer driving a backcountry vehicle and being strong, Rivera was able to arrive at no other conclusions. And that narrowed down the field of suspects to half the men in Grand County.

The deep caws of unseen ravens flying at river level echoed off the red rock walls and caused Rivera to look toward the canyon. The western sky was now filled with an explosion of orange, gold, and pink, with radiating shadows against a dark blue sky. Suddenly two shiny black ravens burst noisily above the canyon walls and soared high into the sky with the sunset as a backdrop. They circled each other playing and squawking, then tumbled and somersaulted down to Rivera's level before leveling off and gliding southward, following the Green River as it slid through Labyrinth Canyon. Rivera's eyes followed them until they disappeared from sight. The scene was another reminder of why he loved the high-desert canyon country, and why he'd left Las Cruces and moved north to Moab. He wished Vivian were here to share the moment, standing next to him, holding his hand. It would have been one of those unforgettable memories they'd have forever.

There was no sense rushing back to the office as it would be quite late by the time he arrived. He decided to remain and enjoy the view for a while longer. That would mean negotiating the primitive road back to the pavement in the dark, but his pickup was certainly capable. It was high-clearance and four-wheel-drive, equipped with a heavy-duty suspension, skid plates, and extra headlights on the roof.

From his vehicle he extracted a folding canvas chair, his windbreaker, two granola bars, and an Aquafina bottle he periodically refilled from his kitchen tap. He unfolded the chair and set it up facing west. Then he slipped on his windbreaker, knowing well how fast the temperature drops in the high desert after sunset. He sat down, began munching on one of the granola bars, and relaxed. His job often took him into the back-country and he'd learned to take advantage of opportunities like this whenever they presented themselves. He stretched out his legs and scanned the deserted expanse of mesa on the other side of the canyon. The solitude and silence of the desert provided him with a comfort unlike anything else. Before long, he felt his body relaxing.

Thirty minutes after the sun had set, the sky became a profusion of dark orange, crimson, and every shade of purple. The faint scent of sagebrush floated on the breeze. Soon, the mesa top began pulsating with the rhythmic sounds of nocturnal desert creatures, signaling the commencement of nightfall. Toads, crickets, cicadas, and beetles began their conversations and flirtations. Now and then, the brush rustled with the movement of a small mammal, foraging for an evening meal, hoping it didn't become one. On the other side of the canyon, an early owl hooted. The night desert was coming alive and all of Rivera's senses were focused on the event.

As darkness gathered and the night grew longer, Venus appeared as a brilliant solitary spot in the sky. Soon thereafter the stars began to appear, first as a few tiny pinpoints of light. As the minutes ticked by, more and more of them could be seen. The change was imperceptible, but slowly the darkness overhead blossomed into an immense skyscape of stars, constellations, and clusters, with an impossibly bright Milky Way bisecting the entire scene.

Rivera scanned the sky and found the Big Dipper. His eyes drew a line upward from the two stars at the far end of the cup and located the North Star. This was something he frequently did, often without conscious thought. It gave him a sense of comfort and reassurance. The universe was intact and everything was still in its place. Things were the way they were supposed to be, regardless of all the man-made craziness on earth.

Rivera's thoughts returned to Vivian. He could see a clear picture of her in his mind. She was five-foot-six with long dark hair and green eyes, a beautiful smile, and the trim athletic look of someone who enjoyed outdoor activities. She was a young-looking twenty-seven years old. For the past ten months, they'd been seeing each other every week or two as their busy schedules permitted. He was definitely hooked. They liked to do many of the same things. Hiking, letter-boxing, and exploring the backcountry in Rivera's old Jeep Wrangler were regular activities for them. They laughed often and enjoyed each other's company. But in some ways she was a mystery. Sometimes she seemed very close, very involved, very much in the present. Other times she seemed distant, almost melancholy. He didn't understand why but he tried to accept her the way she was.

He always enjoyed talking to her about his own life, his family and friends back in Las Cruces, his job as a deputy sheriff, and what he loved about Moab. She was attentive and asked all the right questions. But whenever he tried to get her to talk about her family and friends back in Taos, she seemed to sidestep the question. He figured she was a private person and reluctant to talk about herself. Just the opposite of him. So he learned not to push it. Why spoil the relationship? He felt sure she would open up in time.

He hoped she was the one, that finally his searching had come to an end. But what if she wasn't? Would he ever find what he was looking for? He put that thought out of his mind.

A coyote howled from the other side of the canyon. Another answered. The moon began rising over the

LaSals, flooding the landscape with a soft light. Soon other coyotes joined in the chorus of howling and yipping. To Rivera's ears, it was beautiful music.

He forced his thoughts back to Flanagan's killer. If he were someone from New York with a revenge motive, why would he hide the body? Why not just dump it somewhere in the brush, leave Utah as quickly as possible, and return home? Why drive to the end of this difficult road and carry all those heavy rocks? It didn't make sense. The revenge theory propounded by Reynolds had to be wrong.

Of course, Reynolds himself might have done it. He looked physically capable of carrying the body and the rocks. His motive, of course, wouldn't have been revenge. Instead it would have been his desire for fame and success. If Sam Enderle was right, Reynolds wanted to write a book describing his exploits with Flanagan in New York, ensuring a place for himself in investigative journalism history. He would pretend that he and Flanagan had worked as a team. And Flanagan wouldn't be around to correct the record. As a bonus, the discovery of Flanagan's skeletal remains behind a pile of rocks on a bluff overlooking Labyrinth Canyon would give the story a nice buzz. The book would be in high demand. Maybe even a best seller. But planning such an outcome in advance would involve a lot of uncertainty. What if the body had never been found? There would be no impetus for publishing the book.

Furthermore, Reynolds didn't seem the type who would take big risks in his search for fame or anything else. He couldn't be completely ruled out as a suspect but after visiting the Labyrinth Canyon site, Rivera was more convinced than ever the crime was committed by a local, for a reason connected in some way with one of Flanagan's five files.

13

BART WINSLOW STOOD at the window of his cabin, leaning against the casing, staring out into the darkness and thinking about his life. He watched as intermittent flashes of lightning illuminated the LaSal Mountains. Lately, he often found himself wondering if his life would ever change. Or was he forever stuck in his present situation? Tonight that question weighed heavily on his mind. Things didn't look real promising; in four months he would be thirty and he was still living with his parents.

He needed more income and his cousin Ralph was the key to getting it, but Ralph didn't seem interested in generating a lot of business. If only he would become motivated, Bart's money problem would be solved. Oh well, at least Ralph had gotten the current order for two identities. That would mean ten thousand dollars in Bart's pocket. Not enough for a down payment on a condo, but it was a beginning.

Earlier in the evening, Bart had enjoyed a meal of grilled pork chops, asparagus, and sweet potatoes as only his mother could fix them. The warm apple crumb cake which followed was a delicious surprise made even better by a large scoop of vanilla ice cream sitting next to it on the plate. He took a second plateful of dessert back to the cabin when he left. Living with your parents did have its advantages.

During dinner, with topographic maps spread out on the table, his father had outlined the proposed plans for their hike into Robbers Roost Canyon. He'd planned the exact route, the food and water rations, and the equipment they would need. He'd already begun loading their backpacks. Descending into the canyon would be a challenging hike, but his father was an expert at navigation and exploration. He'd find the best route. For years he'd operated as a backcountry outfitter and knew the Four Corners region as well as anyone. He had a reputation for being the best in the business. Until the day he retired, his services were in high demand from serious hikers, rock climbers, rafters, and hunters. Bart had total confidence in him and loved spending time with him.

He returned to his desk and sat down. Time to get to work. The sooner he finished, the sooner he'd get paid. He unfolded a sheet of paper and studied the notes he'd made during his conversation with Ralph. His goal for tonight was to develop the first identity. This would be the easier of the two since he would be using a name from the bus accident. The death records of the eleven orphans had been deleted years ago so the hard part of the job had already been accomplished. That included the death records of Anthony L. Chester, the name he would use tonight, and the last name of the original eleven. What remained to be done was the creation of a college transcript and a work history.

Chester was about to receive a Bachelor's Degree in Mechanical Engineering. The first step was to identify the target university. Smaller schools were the easiest to hack into because their computers usually had minimal firewall protection. It was a question of economics. Large universities had substantial IT budgets and could afford the most advanced protection for their computer systems. Smaller schools had limited budgets and could afford little more protection than a home computer.

Southwestern Idaho University was such a university. It had an engineering college which was founded in 1956 and offered degrees in electrical, mechanical, and civil engineering. Each year, about one hundred new engineers were graduated. He went to the university's public website and clicked on a button entitled *Alumni*. That took him to a section of the website containing information of interest to previous graduates and, of course, ways they could donate funds to the school. It also included an online version of the quarterly alumni publication called *SIU Magazine.*

He clicked on the most recent copy of the quarterly and located the page that listed alumni obituary notices. He searched for any male graduate in mechanical engineering from the classes of 1981 through 1986. There were no suitable graduates listed in that quarterly, so he reviewed previous quarterlies, working his way back in time. The issue for the fall of 2009 gave him what he was looking for. Francis J. Semmes, a 1983 graduate in mechanical engineering, had passed away on July 1ˢᵗ of 2009. Bart performed a Google search on the name and came up with an obituary in the *Idaho Statesman* newspaper. Semmes had died of a heart attack and left behind a wife, two daughters, and one granddaughter. He was employed by Intermountain Microcircuits Corporation as a Staff Engineer and was a member of the Rotary Club and the Sierra Club. Seemed like a pretty normal life. He wasn't famous for anything and that was good. It was less likely that someone would contact the school and request a copy of his transcript.

Bart's plan was to hack into the university's computer, locate the student transcript files, and substitute the name Anthony L. Chester in place of Francis J. Semmes on Semmes's transcript. After that was accomplished, any request sent to the university for the educational record of Anthony L. Chester, class of 1983, would yield a transcript showing a degree in mechanical engineering had been awarded.

Hacking into this particular computer system turned out to be child's play for Bart. The university website included a page where students and faculty members could log onto the university computer. To log on, a user name and corresponding password were required. He determined the format of user names by going to the "contact us" section of the university's website. There were several contact points listed: the alumni office, admissions office, registrar's office, provost's office, and others. The email addresses were all formatted as: "firstname.lastname@swiu.edu." Normally user names were formatted the same way as email addresses, in this case: "firstname.lastname."

He logged into the computer with the registrar's user-name: samuel.robbins. To fill in the password block, he would employ a trial-and-error method he had developed years ago. More advanced techniques were at his disposal, but he would try this simple attack first. His initial assumption was that the password was alphabetic and six characters long. That was the most common password length so he would start there. If this assumption proved incorrect, he would vary the password length, first by shortening it, then, if necessary, by lengthening it. If none of the password lengths worked, he would repeat the process using hybrid characters, that is, a combination of alphabetic and numeric characters.

He'd written his own software program to generate and transmit all possible password combinations. For six alphabetic characters, there were over three-hundred million combinations, but at a trial-and-error rate of sixty-thousand attempts per second, his computer could input all possible combinations into the target computer in less than two hours. Bart tapped the *input* key and started the process. He speared a piece of apple crumb cake from his plate, forked it into his mouth, and watched intently as his computer "conversed" with the university computer. Within forty minutes, the correct password had been attempted. Now he was through the firewall and into the university's computer. Since the registrar had clearance to access and modify student transcripts, the rest was simple. He performed the name substitution and then checked his work by pulling up Anthony L. Chester's transcript. The result showed a complete listing of Chester's courses and grades, culminating in the award of a Bachelor's Degree in Mechanical Engineering in 1983. His grade point average was a respectable 2.9. Perfect. Bart logged off and rewarded himself with another forkful of cake.

The next order of business was to create a work history from the time Chester graduated from Southwestern Idaho University up to the present. Bart's method for accomplishing this was to list a series of well-known but defunct companies on the resume for the previous work history. He chose Enron Corporation and two of its subsidiaries for this purpose. For the present job he would list a shell consulting company he'd created himself. The company was called Mission Business Consultants. Its specialty, according to its website, was improving the efficiency of client companies. This allowed it to "employ" people with virtually any background. The company could be contacted only by email and would, of course, confirm the employment of Mr. Chester to anyone who inquired.

Upon completion of the project, Bart organized the information into a resume format which he would later fax to Ralph:

Anthony L. Chester
Born in Moab, Grand County, Utah on September 7, 1962
B.S. in Mechanical Engineering, 1983
GPA 2.9
Southwestern Idaho University

1983-1985	Houston Natural Gas Company, Houston, Texas	Field Engineer
1985-1986	InterNorth Corporation, Houston, Texas	Senior Engineer
1987-2001	Enron Corporation, Houston, Texas	Principal Engineer
2001-Present	Mission Business Consultants	Consulting Engineer

Anyone wishing to verify Chester's work history with the first three companies would find it very difficult. Enron went bankrupt in a now-famous financial scandal, and the first two companies were former subsidiaries of Enron. His current employer, Mission Business Consultants, would be most happy to verify his employment and give him a stellar recommendation.

Bart was confident Ralph knew his end of the job well, having done it several times before. His job entailed more than just finding clients. He had to do a lot of hand-holding after the new identity was delivered, guiding the client through several additional steps. He coached them on obtaining a driver's license and a few credit cards to be used for identification purposes. The driver's license would then be used to request, via the internet, a copy of the birth certificate from Salt Lake City. Then the university would be contacted, and a copy of the transcript requested. To establish a personal checking account at a bank, a Social Security number was required. But Bart had instructed Ralph that under no circumstances was the client to contact the Social Security Administration. Even though the SSA might simply accept a copy of the birth certificate as the basis for issuing a social security number, it was too risky. What if someone years ago had already requested a social security number for one of the orphans in order to set up a trust fund? And Homeland Security had so tightened the rules for obtaining Social Security numbers after nine-eleven that it would be taking too great a chance. Instead, Ralph would show the client how to establish a shell company, register it, and request an Employer Identification Number from the IRS. An EIN was acceptable to most banks in place of a social security number for establishing company checking accounts. So a company account would be set up and used by the client in place of a personal checking account. And that would do it. The client would have everything he needed to conduct a normal life using the new identity.

Bart looked at his watch. It was after midnight. Time to hit the sack. He would produce the second resume tomorrow night after work.

14

THE FIRST THING RIVERA learned when he arrived at the office Thursday morning made him very unhappy.

"No photos? He never showed up at all?"

Meredith shook her head. "And he didn't call either."

"Then I'll go find him myself." said Rivera, trying to suppress his irritation and maintain a professional demeanor.

"Manny, do you want me to make some calls to see if he's still registered at one of the motels?"

"Good idea, Meredith. Thanks."

Rivera strode to his office, closed the door, and fell heavily into his chair. He was more than a little annoyed. It wasn't that Reynolds was his top suspect. He wasn't. It wasn't even that Rivera thought the photos were important. So what was it then? He took off his hat and tossed it on the file cabinet. He wondered why Reynolds got under his skin so much. He was not a likeable character, that was for sure. But that wasn't what irritated him. Maybe it was the way some big-city people looked down on small-town folks as though they were less intelligent, less important. He'd seen that before as a young city cop in Las Cruces. He remembered a time years ago when he was giving a speeding citation to a driver from Los Angeles in a late-model Lexus. The man's wife wanted to know if they were really expected to pay the fine. After all, they lived in California and wouldn't ever be coming back to this backwater town again. She was laughing in a condescending manner as she said it.

Whatever the reason for the no-show, Reynolds would get a piece of his mind. Maybe the threat of a night or two in jail would improve the man's manners.

However all that would have to wait until later. His priorities for this morning were to interview Skip Kennison and find out if he had any idea why the newspaper article about his wedding had found its way into February's files. After that, he would pay another visit to the Moab district office of the Utah Department of Health to ask Linda Anderson a few follow-up questions.

At Kennison's Real Estate office he learned that Kennison was in Colorado on an elk hunting trip. He was scheduled to return tomorrow. The interview would have to wait, so Rivera decided to do the next best thing. He would visit Kennison's best man, Meriwether Williams, who was also in the photograph that accompanied the wedding article. Perhaps Williams would have some idea why Flanagan had had an interest in Kennison.

Rivera found a parking spot on Main Street directly in front of the iconic two-story Uranium Building. He entered and walked up the staircase to the second floor where several small offices were located. He found the door marked Seven Star Investments and knocked. He heard the shuffling of feet.

A moment later, a man opened the door and smiled pleasantly. "Good morning," he said, looking over his glasses. "Can I help you?"

"Good morning, Mr. Williams. I'm Deputy Sheriff Manny Rivera. I'd like to ask you a few questions about an investigation I'm conducting."

"Sure, Deputy. Come on in," said Williams.

The man looked to be in his mid-forties. He was slightly hunched over and supported himself with a cane. His close-cropped hair was dark brown, and he had a full beard. His brown eyes were soft, almost doe-like. He was wearing khaki slacks and a short sleeve shirt. His arms and upper body were toned and muscular but one of his legs appeared damaged.

Williams motioned for Rivera to have a seat as he limped around the desk and lowered himself into his chair.

Rivera sat down and surveyed the room. Alongside the desk was a small table with two laptop computers, one displaying graphs of some sort, the other showing columns of numbers. The numbers were being periodically updated, some switching from red to green and back again. Built-in bookshelves on Rivera's left were filled with books, colorful chunks of petrified wood, framed photographs, bronze sculptures, and trophies of various sizes. On his right were several filing cabinets. Hanging on the wall above them were two oil paintings which Rivera recognized as Wendell Cosgrove's.

"I see you've got some of Wendell Cosgrove's paintings," said Rivera.

Williams smiled. "Yeah, I'm a big fan of his. The wife and I have a few more of his paintings at home." He gestured toward the bookshelves. "I've also got a complete set of his shaman sculptures on the shelf over there."

Rivera glanced at them. They looked like the ones he'd seen in Cosgrove's studio. Interested, he got out of his chair, and walked over to take a closer look. The sculptures were ten-inch high bronzes. They were modeled after shaman petroglyphs chipped into rock faces in the surrounding backcountry by ancient-Indian cultures. Each shaman wore a headdress of some type and had a broad torso with stick-like arms and legs. He recognized one of them as Moab Man, a petroglyph which was unique because it had one arm raised up and one arm down. Moab was the only place in the entire Four Corners region where such a petroglyph could be found. Thus the name Moab Man.

Rivera studied the collection. "Wendell does good work," he said as he returned to his chair.

"Yeah, I love his art. He's a real asset to the community." Williams turned his head and studied the computer displays for a few seconds, then returned his attention to Rivera. "You said you had some questions you wanted to ask me."

"Right." Rivera took out his notepad and ball-point pen. He clicked the pen open with his thumb. "Did you know February Flanagan?"

"I'd heard of him around town but never met him personally." Williams leaned back in his chair and folded his forearms across his chest. "People said he was a drinker. Claire and I aren't drinking people and don't normally associate with those who do."

"Claire is your wife?"

"Yeah. That's her in the photograph." He pointed a finger at a framed photo on his desk. "She's the best thing that ever happened to me."

Rivera shot a quick glance at Claire. She was a plain-looking woman with dark eyes and sharp features. Her hair was parted in the middle and tied back tightly on her head.

"Flanagan kept some files in the trunk of his car. One of them contained a clipping from the *Times-Independent*. It was an article about Skip Kennison's wedding. The article included a photograph of the bride and groom flanked by you and Claire."

Williams looked surprised. "Claire and I stood up for Skip and Kay at their wedding. But I have no idea why Flanagan would have had an interest in us. Skip will be back in town tomorrow. Maybe he could tell you something."

"May I ask the nature of your business?"

"Investments. I manage money for my family, my wife's family, and a few close friends. It's closed to the public. Keeps everything simple that way. I have no employees. Not even a secretary." He gestured toward the laptop computers. "I do all my research from this office."

"You mean like stocks and bonds?

"Stocks, bonds, real estate, and a few small venture capital projects."

Rivera nodded, but knowing little about investing, he couldn't come up with a sensible comment. So he closed his notepad and wrapped up the interview by asking Williams about the trophies in the bookshelves.

"They're for kayaking. I managed to win a few of the Colorado River races. It's great exercise. And fortunately, it's something I can do even with this bum leg."

Rivera studied two framed photographs next to the trophies, one of a smiling Williams sitting in a red and white kayak, the other showing Williams on a river bank supporting himself with his cane and accepting a trophy. "I'll have to try it someday," Rivera said. "I haven't rafted the rivers at all, much less kayaked them."

"You'd love it. The Colorado is a perfect river for kayaking. And it's so close to town. Why don't you come watch one of our races sometime? Afterwards I'd be happy to show you how it's done."

"Thanks, I'd like that very much."

Rivera shook hands with Williams and departed.

As he descended the staircase and exited the Uranium Building, he formed a mental picture of Williams kayaking down the Colorado. He couldn't flex his knee but his muscular arms and shoulders probably more than offset that disadvantage. He decided to accept William's invitation. He'd show up for the next scheduled race. And he'd see if Vivian wanted to go along.

Rivera could fathom no reason for Flanagan's interest in the weddings. A sense he was getting nowhere began to seep into Rivera's thoughts. Maybe this old crime would never get solved.

He drove to the Health Department office, noticing the peaks of the LaSals were now white. The thunderstorm that passed over the mountains yesterday had deposited a layer of snow at the higher altitudes. An early sign that winter wasn't far off.

Linda Anderson was in her office.

Rivera handed her the 2005 organization chart. "Linda, take a look at this organization chart. Does it ring any kind of a bell? Anything at all?"

She put on her reading glasses and studied the chart. A long moment passed. She shook her head. "The only thing that stands out is how few people on this old chart still work here. Let's see. We have nine-teen employees now just as we did back then. But there are only five people left of the nineteen listed on the chart. That's me and four others. I didn't realize our turnover rate was so high. Let's take a walk out into the work area and I'll point out the employees who were here back then."

He followed her out of the office. Anderson pointed to a grey-haired lady sitting at a desk by the front window. That's Lilly Ogden. She's in charge of medical records. She was here back then."

Lilly looked up and smiled. Next, Anderson pointed to a young man hunched over his desk, talking intently on the telephone. "And that's Jude Jeffers. He's in charge of scheduling and appointments." She pointed to the far corner. "Yvonne Broderick over there oversees infectious disease prevention and cure."

"In the back behind the partition is our computer system." They moved toward the rear of the room and glanced around the partition. She pointed. "That's Bart Winslow, our computer guru. He was also working here back then." Winslow looked up, saw them, and quickly returned his attention to the manual on his desk.

They returned to Anderson's office. "That's every-one from the current staff who was working here back in 2005. I don't know what else I can tell you, Manny. As I said, Feb was in here often asking ques-tions, but I can't think of anything he was particularly interested in. He seemed interested in everything we were doing."

After a quick lunch at Wendy's, Rivera drove to the Desert Sky Lodge, a two-story motel on Main Street. Meredith had informed him William Reynolds was registered there. He parked, took a deep breath, and got out of his truck. He walked to the front desk and tapped the bell sitting on the countertop. A clerk appeared from a side office.

"Hi. Can I help you?"

"I'd like to speak with William Reynolds. Can you tell me which room he's in?"

"Yes, Sir. One moment please." The clerk tapped a few keys on a computer keyboard and studied the monitor.

"He's in Room One-Twelve." The clerk pointed out the window. "It's down that walkway about halfway to the end of the building"

"Thanks."

Rivera pushed open the office door and proceeded down the walkway, glancing at the descending numbers on the doors. Suddenly he heard a scream. A housekeeper rushed from one of the rooms with a horror-stricken look on her face. She ran around her cleaning cart up to Rivera and grabbed his arm with both hands. She was shaking.

"Mr. Policeman, Mr. Policeman! There's a man on the floor in there. Room One-Twelve. I think he's dead."

15

BART WINSLOW SAT in his pickup in the Health Department parking lot in the shade of a large Russian olive tree. A breeze passing through the open windows of his vehicle cooled his face. He took a bite from the ham sandwich his mother had made him for lunch and watched a cowbird hopping across the asphalt, chasing after a fluttering moth.

He was wondering what Linda Anderson had been discussing with the deputy this morning. He'd seen him around town before but didn't know him personally. His name was Rivera. He seemed like a nice enough guy with a friendly intelligent face and a rugged Hispanic handsomeness the ladies always seemed to take note of. Bart hadn't been able to hear what they were talking about over the music of Pink Floyd's *Dark Side of the Moon* emanating from the iPOD buds in his ears. Linda had definitely been pointing Bart out to the deputy. Saying something about him. Surely the deputy wasn't on to what he was doing. Heck, there was no one in town with the technical know-how to understand his little scheme. A few more cowbirds glided into the parking lot and landed. They walked jerkily, pecking at unseen morsels.

He picked up his cell phone and dialed Ralph in Newark.

"Ralph, it's Bart."

"Hi, cousin. You finished already?"

"No, I'm still working on it. I finished the first one last night. I'll work on the second one tonight. But that's not what I wanted to talk to you about."

"What did you want to talk about?"

"Two things. First of all, I want us to raise our price. We should double or even triple it." He heard a sigh on the other end of the line.

"What's the second thing?"

"I want you to step up the marketing. I need money for a down payment on a condo. A lot of money. Houses in Moab are expensive."

"Okay, cousin, I'll step up the marketing."

Bart didn't like Ralph's tone of voice. There was a total absence of enthusiasm. "With all your connections, can't you put more effort into this? It's good money."

Ralph hesitated. "Listen Bart, you know I'm doing things for other people. Things you don't want to know about. I need to keep a low profile. Can't put a sign on the side of my car. *Phony Identities for Sale.* These other people ain't like you, cousin. If I screw up and expose them in the process, there would be serious consequences. Understand?"

"Yeah, I understand. Maybe I need another partner." He terminated the call.

Irritated, he sat there, thinking about what he'd just said. He took the last bite of his ham sandwich and chewed it slowly. Maybe another partner wasn't such a bad idea. Not that he'd end it with Ralph. Ralph held up his end of the operation real well. He just didn't generate enough volume. Cowbirds continued landing in the parking lot. Now there were dozens of them, waddling and pecking. What if Bart had partners in other large cities? Los Angeles, Houston, Chicago. There should be a high demand for new identities in any large city. There was no reason not to have several partners. He would give that some serious thought.

He cranked his pickup to life and the cowbirds rose in unison, flying off in every direction. He pulled out of the parking lot and drove over to the new condo development. He stared at the condos, picturing his vehicle parked in one of the driveways. Not the piece of junk he was driving today. A brand-new Jeep. He got out of his truck and began exploring one of the units under construction. He paused in each room, trying to picture how he would arrange his furniture, soon realizing his hand-me-downs would look totally out of place. Hell, he'd need to buy new furniture too. If only he could afford to do it all. He decided then and there he would begin finding new partners. Unfortunately, that would take time. Time to find them, check them out, train them. Damn, it seemed like it would take forever.

His thoughts drifted back to the time two years ago when he'd asked Irma at the library if she'd like to go to the movies with him. She'd smiled and asked if he was still living at home with his parents. He'd said no, he had his own place behind their house. She raised her eyebrows and produced a 'you've-got-to-be-kidding' expression. He remembered standing there, feeling his face turn red, not knowing what to say. Ever since then, he avoided going into the library for fear of running into her again and reliving the ridicule. She was cute and smart and had long dark hair. With a new condo and a new Jeep, maybe he'd stand a chance with her.

He got back into his truck and sat there, trying to relax and think things through carefully. Ralph had always called him a genius. He was right about that. Bart had never met his equal in the realm of computer science. If only Ralph were more aggressive, they could both be wealthy. He didn't want to push his cousin to the point where he'd get in trouble. He liked Ralph. He didn't understand him or even trust him completely, but he sure didn't want anything bad to happen to him. He started the pickup, relieved to hear the engine kick in on the first try. He glanced up and down the street, made a u-turn, and headed back to the office. Clearly, acquiring additional partners was the answer.

As he drove, it occurred to Bart that he didn't really know for sure how much Ralph was charging the clients. Maybe Ralph had already raised the price and neglected to tell his partner about it.

16

RIVERA REREAD THE CRIME scene reports, tossed them onto his desk, and looked at his watch. It was after seven o'clock. The whole day was gone and now his theory that Flanagan had been killed because of an investigation he'd been conducting in Moab had been turned upside down. The murder of William Reynolds had changed everything. With both victims from New York City, it now appeared the motive might indeed be related to something that had happened back east.

The crime scene investigation at the motel had been completed with the help of the Moab Police Department and the Utah State Police crime lab in Price. Time of death was estimated at midnight. Reynolds' body was found in his motel room face down on the floor. According to the Medical Examiner's report, he'd been shot in the temple with a single 25-caliber slug. In addition, his nose had been broken. No one had been seen entering or leaving Reynolds's room. The slug turned out to be a match for the one that had killed February Flanagan. And the photos Reynolds had been showing around town were nowhere to be found. The general theory was that the killer had knocked on the motel room door and when Reynolds opened it, the killer slugged him, closed the door, and fired a bullet into his head. The killer then grabbed the file containing the pictures, left the room, and wiped his prints off the doorknob.

Rivera leaned back, hoisted his feet onto his desk, and clasped his hands behind his head. Now he had to rethink everything.

The same gun had been used to kill both February Flanagan and William Reynolds, most likely fired by the same person. The killing had the earmarks of a professional hit. A single shot to the head. The 25-caliber pistol was a favorite in the underworld for up-close killing. When fired, it made less noise than a 38-caliber or a 9-mm discharge. And it was less messy. The slug entered the skull and usually did not exit. Since no one at the motel had heard a gunshot, it was presumed a sound suppressor had been used. That also suggested a professional job.

Perhaps Reynolds had been right. Maybe someone from New York with a revenge motive had come to Moab and killed Flanagan. And maybe Reynolds was killed in the mistaken belief he had assisted Flanagan in his investigations. But if that were true, why wait until Reynolds was in Moab? Why not kill him while he was in New York?

Rivera yawned, got up from his chair, and walked down the hall to the break room. Bradshaw was still in his office but everyone else except the night dispatcher was either out on patrol or had gone home. He inserted two quarters into the cold-drink vending machine and pressed a button. A can of Dr. Pepper clunked out. He opened it, took a gulp, and returned to his office just in time to get a call from Chris Carey.

Carey had two things to report. First, he'd found another article about the bus accident in a weekly Castle Dale newspaper that had ceased publication back in the eighties. Unlike the *Salt Lake Tribune* article, this one listed the names of all eleven orphans. Carey slowly read the list over the phone, pausing between each name presumably to give Rivera time to write it down. Rivera didn't have the heart to tell him he'd already gotten the information from the gravestones, but he was impressed with Carey's tenacity and research skills. The second piece of information was bad news.

After he hung up the phone, Rivera walked down the hall to Sheriff Bradshaw's office and sat down in one of the visitor's chairs. This morning's issue of the weekly *Times-Independent* was sitting in the center of the sheriff's desk. The story about the discovery of February Flanagan's body last Saturday was, of course, the lead article. The headline read: *Murdered Man's Body Found in Backcountry.*

Bradshaw tapped the newspaper with his forefinger. "Manny, we need to wrap up the Flanagan case quickly, before the tourists start worrying about how safe they are in the Moab backcountry and decide to go to Escalante or Kanab instead." He pushed himself out of his chair, walked over to the window, and stared out into the darkness for a long moment. "Of course, I'm assuming that solving the Flanagan case also solves the Reynolds case. If that's wrong, then we really have a mess on our hands."

"I'm afraid it's even worse than you think. Do you know Chris Carey, the retired journalist who used to work for the *Times-Independent?*"

Bradshaw turned to face Rivera. "Sure, I know him."

"I just got a call from him. He told me the information about Flanagan being severely beaten before he was shot has come to the attention of the newspaper. Somehow our little secret leaked out. They intend to keep silent about it, but only until the next issue comes out. One week from today."

Bradshaw furrowed his brow, returned to his desk, and lowered himself into his chair. "And if they were a daily newspaper, they'd have kept quiet about it for exactly one day. I should have known better than to try to keep anything secret in this town." He leaned back in his chair. "At least we have a week. Okay, Manny, bring me up to date."

Rivera spent the next twenty minutes running through the facts of the case, starting with his initial review of the Flanagan case file and ending with the results of the motel crime scene investigation. "After I found the five files in the trunk of Flanagan's car, I was fairly certain he was killed because of something he was investigating here in Moab. But after learning that Reynolds was killed with the same gun, I'm not so sure. Now it seems there has to be a New York City connection. I've got to rethink the whole thing."

Bradshaw nodded and was silent for a long moment. "Sometimes it helps to take a step back from the details and try to see the bigger picture. You know, take a larger view."

Rivera sat at his desk, office door closed, feeling a sense of urgency and hoping he would find a way to break the case. He had a high degree of respect and admiration for his boss and didn't want to disappoint him. He thought about what Bradshaw had said. *Take a larger view.* The sheriff was considered one of the finest investigative minds in the state. He was often invited to law enforcement conferences to lecture on the application of logic, inference, and chronology in criminal investigations. But what the heck did he mean by *Take a larger view?* Rivera thought he'd already been doing that. Keeping an open mind. Considering all the possibilities. Narrowing them down to a few. Pursuing the most likely. He decided to start the whole thought process over again.

He polished off the Dr. Pepper and forced himself to concentrate. The two killings were linked by the same gun and, almost certainly, the same killer. Possibly a hired professional. The motivation was most likely the result of a past or present investigation conducted by Flanagan. If everything Sam Enderle had said was accurate, it was unlikely Reynolds was involved in the investigation. Maybe there was a perception or belief by someone that Reynolds had been part of Flanagan's investigation. Maybe Reynolds's pretensions had gotten him killed. Rivera decided to advance his thinking on the premise that the motivation was tied primarily to a Flanagan investigation and that Reynolds had been collateral damage in some way.

There were a number of possibilities. The first was that Flanagan was killed for something he'd done years ago in New York. The revenge motive. If that were the case, the question of "Why move those heavy rocks?" still hung there unanswered. And if Reynolds was also to be killed, why not do it back in New York? Why wait till he came to Moab? Maybe Reynolds did something in Moab to trigger the need for his elimination. If so, showing the pictures around town was most probably the reason. But that would mean that in a period of two days, word had gotten back to New York about Reynolds and the pictures, a decision had been made to kill him, and a hit man dispatched to find him and do the evil deed. That also implied someone in Moab would have recognized the importance of the pictures and made the call to New York. The chronology seemed like a stretch.

A second possibility was that Rivera was on the right track in the first place. Flanagan had been killed because of an investigation he'd been conducting in Moab. In this case, hiding the body would make more sense. Locals would have simply assumed Flanagan had left town and there would be no investigation. The files in the trunk of his car still seemed to be a sensible avenue to pursue. But then Reynolds had been killed by the same gun. Could the killer be living in Moab? If he was, he would certainly have been worried about the pictures. He had no way of knowing for sure whether his photo was included in the stack. So perhaps the killing was a just-in-case preemptive action to take the photo file out of circulation.

A third possibility was that Flanagan and Reynolds were killed for totally unrelated reasons, but that the same hit man had been hired to do the job, coincidentally, by two different people in New York. Highly improbable.

Rivera explored three or four other scenarios before he decided he was too tired to think clearly. He let out a very audible yawn and dropped the case file into his briefcase.

On the drive home, he had the feeling he was getting nowhere. Spinning his wheels. He would get a good night's sleep and start fresh in the morning. Think everything through again. And now there was the added pressure of the newspaper's plan to release the gory details of Flanagan's murder next week.

On top of all that, he realized his date with Vivian Ramos in two days was probably in serious jeopardy.

17

BART WINSLOW HAD SPENT a good part of Thursday afternoon sitting in front of his workstation at the Health Department, pretending to be working on department business but actually developing a strategy for creating the second false identity. Now, in the quiet evening hours, with supper behind him, it was time to execute the plan he'd come up with during the day. He sat down at his roll-top desk and switched on his laptop. Without the benefit of another name from the bus accident, he would have to start from scratch, find a usable name, and delete the corresponding death records.

The essence of the problem was twofold. First, he had to identify a male who was born and died young in Grand County and who would have been in his late forties or early fifties today, had he lived. And second, the deceased had to have no kin who might, at some future date, request a copy of his death certificate. Such a request would be fatal to Bart's business. And it might trigger an investigation that would put him behind bars. That meant the deceased had to have no living parents or siblings. Having died at an early age, he would, of course, have had no spouse or children.

Years ago, Bart had written a special program and loaded it into his office computer. The software allowed him to connect to his office system via the internet from his personal laptop. As a result, he could sit at home and operate remotely from his personal laptop, just as though he were sitting in front of his terminal in the office. He connected to the office computer and typed in the access code which then connected him to the computer system at the Office of Vital Records in Salt Lake City. A blank death certificate form appeared on his screen. He clicked on box 13f, the zip code of the deceased, and typed in XyZvW. He hit the enter button. The covert program he'd installed recognized the special characters in the zip-code field and allowed him to pass through the firewall into the applications software part of the system.

In accordance with his plan, he executed a search of the death certificate database, requesting a listing of all males who had died in Grand County during the early nineteen-sixties at age three or younger. The system produced a list of sixteen names. Using these names as a starting point, he searched for their birth certificates, eliminating those who were not born in Grand County. That dropped the usable total to nine. From the birth records of these nine, he identified the names of their parents. Then he searched for the death records of the parents. If both parents were dead, the name of the deceased child remained as a possible candidate. All others were dropped from the list. That left six names. Now he had to check for siblings.

To do this, he disconnected from the Office of Vital Statistics computer and searched the internet for the parents' names, looking for their obituaries in Utah newspaper archives. The process was time consuming. When he found their obits, he studied them, looking for the existence of other children. In the end, three of the names on the list had had parents with no other children. These three formed his final list.

It had taken him five hours to complete the work, but it was well worth the effort. Not only did he have a second identity for the current job, he also had two more he could use on future jobs.

He selected one of the names, Jeffrey B. Lynch, as the second identity. The next step was to delete his death records. He reconnected to the Office of Vital Statistics computer, again penetrated the firewall, and substituted a bogus name for Lynch's in the master directory of the death record database. Now, no one would ever find the stored image of Lynch's death record. It was virtually non-existent. That done, he logged off the Salt Lake City computer. Next, he searched the Moab Health Department computer system for any reference to Lynch's death and deleted that as well. Tomorrow or some day next week, he would find a reason to unlock the file room in the rear of the building, remove the copy of Lynch's paper death certificate, and destroy it. After that, there would be a birth record on file for Jeffrey B. Lynch but no record whatsoever of his death, assuming no one ever checked the cold storage files containing the original paper death certificate in Salt Lake City.

Having a name for the second identity, Bart initiated the process for acquiring a college degree. He found a small college in southern Indiana which awarded Bachelor's Degrees in Business Administration with accounting majors, hacked into the school's computer system, and secured a transcript and degree for Mr. Lynch using the name-substitution technique. Then he constructed a past work history from defunct but recognizable corporations. Mr. Lynch's current job was listed as a consulting accountant for Mission Business Consultants. Finally, Bart organized the information into a resume format. The job was done.

It had been a long night and Bart went right to bed. Tired but not sleepy, he lay there with mixed emotions, satisfied and proud he'd been able to successfully complete the current project but deeply concerned about his partner's diligence. Worse than that, he was becoming increasingly suspicious of his trustworthiness.

18

AFTER FEEDING HIS GUPPIES, Rivera retrieved a can of beer from his refrigerator and pulled on the ring tab. He took a swig and sat down at the kitchen table. It was nearly nine o'clock and he was famished. He opened the sack of groceries he'd bought at City Market and removed a box of fried chicken, a small tub of cole slaw, and two brownies.

As he ate, a cloud of frustration and doubt hung over him. Had the last four days had been a total waste? His thoughts drifted back to Bradshaw's counsel. *Take a larger view.* Tired after a long day, he tried to do just that. He ran through the facts of the case over and over in his mind but nothing clicked. Not a single idea. Maybe the "larger view" business didn't apply to this case.

After eating dinner, he went into the living room, inserted *The Milagro Beanfield War* disk into his DVD player, and fell heavily onto the couch with a second can of beer. About thirty minutes into the movie, he began to feel relaxed. He'd managed to put Flanagan and Reynolds out of his mind, if only for a little while.

The story was beautiful, even delicate, and some of the characters in the movie reminded him of his family and friends back in Las Cruces. Suddenly he missed them terribly and felt a longing to be with them, talking, laughing, telling stories, and kidding one another. He particularly missed his grandmother's world-class enchiladas and his late-night conversations with his grandfather about life and its purpose. He enjoyed staying with his parents and visiting with his sisters and brothers. He'd talked to them all by phone or email but hadn't seen them since July. He was overdue for a visit. Unfortunately, his next trip would have to wait until the Flanagan/Reynolds matter was resolved.

The telephone rang. He reluctantly pressed the pause button on the DVD remote, walked into his bedroom, and picked up the phone.

"Hello." He stifled a yawn.

"Hello, I'd like to speak to Deputy Sheriff Manny Rivera, please."

"Speaking."

"Deputy, my name is Frank McKelvey. From New York City. I'm returning your call."

"Oh, yes. Thanks for calling back, Mr. McKelvey. As I said in my message, I'm investigating the murder of February Flanagan. We're trying to get all the background information on him that we can. I found your business card in with some of his files. Can you tell me what kind of relationship you had with him?"

"First of all, let me apologize for not getting back to you sooner. I've been gone from the office for a few days working on a case down in Baltimore. Just got back this evening. It's nearly midnight here and I'm still in the office trying to catch up. I didn't know Feb was dead until I played back your message. Poor guy. I can't say I'm surprised, though. He always lived on the edge. What happened?"

"We found his remains last weekend, buried under a rock ledge out by a remote canyon. Been dead for three years. Bullet to the back of the head."

"Damn." There was a pause. "I sure liked that fellow. He did me a lot of favors over the years. Helped in some of my private investigations, gave me lots of good advice. He was about twenty-five years older than me so he was sort of like a mentor. And he provided me with free tickets to the Knicks game whenever the Celtics were in town. Floor seats for me and Gloria. She's from Boston. Anyway, I owed him big time. But he never asked for anything in return. Until one day about three-and-a-half years ago, that is. He called and asked me to do some background research on several people he was interested in. Gave me a list of names. Feb knew I had good contacts all over the country through the Association of Professional Investigators. Our members have friends in all the right places, if you know what I mean. Good connections. I did the job and called him a few weeks later with the results. End of story."

Rivera was now wide awake. "Do you remember the names, what you found out about them, so forth?"

"Hold on. I figured you'd ask me that, so I dug out the file before I called you. I've got it right here in front of me."

Rivera heard the shuffling of papers.

"Okay, here are the notes from his call to me. Let's see. He gave me eleven names and birthdates. All born in Grand County, Utah. He wanted to know anything I could find out about them. Want me to read the names to you?"

"Yes, please." Rivera had a feeling he already knew the names. He pulled his notepad out of his shirt pocket and turned to the page where he'd written down the names of the eleven orphans buried in the Thompson Springs Cemetery. He checked off each name as McKelvey spoke.

"Okay, here they are: Harry Dixon, Leonard Simpson, Miriam Bell, Richard Williams, Mary Bresnahan, Milton Winters, Lee Roy Hicks, Edith Bellinger, Anthony Chester, Stanley Cook, and Douglas Campbell. Got all that?"

"Got it."

"Now, do you want the birthdates?"

"Please."

Rivera listened as McKelvey went down the list of names and ticked off the corresponding birth dates.

The dates were exactly as Rivera had transcribed from the grave markers.

"Can you tell me what you found out about each of them?"

"Sure. I only found information on five of them. But of those five, they all seemed to have one thing in common: a false identity. I don't know what Feb was getting himself into, but each of the five had a very interesting story. Do you want to hear all this? It'll take a while."

"I sure do. Every bit of it." He sat down on his bed.

"Harry L. Dixon was an alias for a man whose real name is Vladimir Krivichi. He was an illegal immigrant from Belarus. He established a business in the Bronx called Bruckner Delivery Company. The place was actually a front for distributing illegal drugs. He was busted by the New York City cops in 2005 and sentenced to twelve years in the pen, after which he'll be deported.

"Next is Mary A. Bresnahan. This one is interesting. In 2006, a guy named Ted Broderick buys life insurance for his supposed live-in girlfriend named Mary Bresnahan. She supposedly goes sailing alone in the Long Island Sound during rough weather. A squall comes up. She never returns. He claims she drowned and the insurance company can't prove otherwise. He collects one hundred fifty thousand. Did she ever really exist? Who knows?

"The third one is Milton Winters. Very similar to the Bresnahan case. Another boating accident, this time in the Pacific. A lady named Ellie Weiss from Santa Monica collects three hundred and twenty grand.

"The fourth one, Lee Roy Hicks, was an alias used by a hood from Chicago named Danny O'Rourke. He was wanted in three states on several counts of armed robbery and assault. The heat was on. So he changed his identity and laid low for a year in Cleveland. But his old habits of beating people up and taking their money got him in trouble again. He was arrested in Chicago and sentenced to twenty-five years in the Illinois State Pen.

"The last one is Edith Bellinger, an alias for an illegal immigrant by the name of Juana Baeza from Monterey, Mexico. Arrested in Houston for extortion and assault. Deported.

"That's everything I was able to get for Feb at that point in time. I asked him if he wanted me to keep pursuing the other names. He said no, he'd gotten what he needed. He thanked me and hung up."

"Did you hear from him again after that?"

"No, that was the last time we talked."

"Did you find a death certificate for any of the eleven names Flanagan gave you? Or any kind of reference to a death?"

"We didn't check for death certificates. There was no reason to. But if any of those names had shown up in the obituaries and they'd had the right birth date, we'd have probably caught it. We searched for all eleven names in all fifty states."

After Rivera hung up the phone, he retrieved his briefcase from the kitchen and went to his desk in the second bedroom. He extracted February's five files from his briefcase and spread them out across his desk. He nodded his head and smiled. He knew he had a tendency to jump to conclusions and despite his best efforts to overcome that flaw, he'd done it again. He'd been trying to narrow down his focus to a single one of the five files. Now he could see that four and possibly all five of the files were related to a single investigation Flanagan had been conducting. He sat back, thinking about what Bradshaw had said. *Take a larger view.* His boss had been right.

The files entitled *Insurance Fraud, Illegal Immigration,* and *Bus Accident 1968* were obviously connected. Two of the names McKelvey had run down were involved in insurance fraud and two were illegal immigrants. All five had assumed names taken from the orphans killed in the 1968 bus accident. And the Health Department was responsible for birth and death certificates, so the file entitled *Utah Department of Health, Moab Office* was tied into the first three. He couldn't yet see any connection with the contents of the *Wedding Article* file but maybe after he interviewed Kennison tomorrow, that too would become clear.

He decided to visit Linda Anderson first thing in the morning. Armed with this new information, maybe she could help him make sense of things.

19

THE SOUND OF A dog barking in the distance came through the open window of Bart's cabin and awakened him from a night of fitful sleep. He untangled himself from the bed sheets, rolled over, and squinted at the red numerals on the alarm clock next to his bed. The display read 4:14 A.M. A very light sleeper, he knew his chances of dozing off again were somewhere between slim and none. So he lay there, as he often did on sleepless nights, not fighting his insomnia. Instead, he used the time as an opportunity to think about whatever came into his mind. When he first started having trouble sleeping, it worried him. And worrying made it even harder to fall asleep. Then he discovered that these periods of sleeplessness before daylight were the best times for clear thinking. His mind was relaxed and open to new thoughts and ideas. He learned to just lie there and allow his mind to take him wherever it wanted.

Not surprisingly, his first thoughts were about Irma at the library. They usually were. In a way, she was his

main objective. If he were able to attract her, then, probably, everything else in his life would be okay. Moving
out of his parents' cabin and into a new condo would
be the first step in sparking her interest. That would
require money. And, of course, he would need to get
rid of that junky pickup he was driving and replace
it with something cool. A flashy Jeep Rubicon with a
jacked-up backcountry suspension and big tires would
be about right. That would require more money. And
he'd have to lose some weight. He loved his mother's
cooking but eating two or three helpings of it every
night was probably the reason he was overweight. Living
in his own condo and eating his own cooking for a
few months would probably reduce his belt size. The
thesis was clear. Every one of his goals in life revolved
around making enough money to upgrade his standard
of living.

That thought led him to reflect on the two new identities he'd just created. What a lovely business. Identities
made to order. They cost him nothing to produce and
sold for thousands. He was brilliant to have thought of
it. He'd call Ralph later in the morning and tell him
he'd be sending the results of their latest project by fax.
And while he had him on the phone, he'd again press
him about raising prices. Surely a new ID was worth
more than ten thousand dollars.

The dog barked again. Bart always marveled at how
far sound traveled in the cool night air of the high

desert. And how clear and sharp it was. It almost had an echo quality to it. He wondered what was bothering the dog at this hour.

He rearranged the blanket so his feet were covered and continued his ruminations. The solution to all his problems seemed clear. Increased prices and more sales would allow him to buy the condo and the truck and move out of the cabin. Winning Irma's heart wouldn't be far behind.

This line of thinking caused a new worry to surface. Something that had been lurking in the back of Bart's mind for days. What if Ralph was already charging the clients a higher fee? What if he'd been lying to his partner all along about how much he collected for each new identity? It was entirely possible. And Bart would never know. Ralph was the sole point of contact with the clients. As the minutes ticked by, he tumbled this troubling thought over and over in his mind. And the more he dwelled on it, the more convinced he became that Ralph was selling the identities for a lot more than ten thousand apiece. That was the only logical reason Ralph wouldn't agree to a price increase. Bart was the brains of the operation and his cousin was playing him for a damned sucker. Filled with agitation, he was now wide awake. He sat up and swung his feet onto the floor. He had to find out for sure.

He turned on the lamp and slipped into a T-shirt, a pair of shorts, and his sneakers. He climbed down the ladder from the loft, made his way to the bathroom, splashed cold water on his face, and brushed his teeth. Then he went to his roll-top desk and sat down in front of his laptop.

He pondered for a moment. Then he hit a few keystrokes and retrieved from the computer's memory the list of names he'd previously used for false identities. Ten names and birthdates flashed onto the screen. His plan was to perform an exhaustive internet search on each name in hopes of finding a way to contact them. He'd call anonymously from a pay phone. He'd ask them directly how much they'd paid for their identity. Exactly how he'd intimidate them into providing that information, he hadn't yet figured out. He'd worry about that later. Why hadn't he thought of this before? It would answer the question once and for all of whether his cousin was cheating him.

He searched for the first name on the list: Harry L. Dixon, born May 6, 1960. He used the Google and Bing search engines, as well as several others he was familiar with, to scan the World Wide Web. While painstakingly checking all the search references for Dixon's name, he found several newspaper articles where he was mentioned. He learned the man was an illegal immigrant and currently in prison for distributing drugs in the Bronx. No point in trying to contact him.

He continued down the list of names, searching the internet, trying to learn what he could about each of them. His knee bounced impatiently as he awaited the results of each search. About the time the birds started chirping outside, he made a startling discovery. One of the names on the list corresponded to a man living in Moab. He recognized the name instantly. The date of birth was also a match. The man was well known in the community and reputed to be quite wealthy. He sat back and considered this new revelation. Then he smiled.

Now he had two options. As originally planned, he could try to find out from the man what he'd paid for the false ID. Or, even better, he could approach him about a loan for a down payment on the condo. Not with the threat of exposure but rather as a partner in crime. Members of the same brotherhood.

Of course he would be exposing himself in the process. If things didn't go his way with the loan, he sure wouldn't want a Moab resident knowing what he was up to in the Health Department. He got up, walked to the window, and peered outside. The western sky was a mass of stars and the peaks of the LaSal Mountains to the east were outlined in a predawn golden hue. Was there a way for Bart to do this without revealing his identity? Maybe there was. He could call the man anonymously and see how he reacted to the suggestion of a loan. Feel him out. If the reaction was negative, nothing would be lost. He would forget the whole idea of borrowing money. Then he could fall back on Plan B and try to find out how much the man had paid Ralph for the false identity.

On the other hand, the man might be more than willing to cooperate. Maybe he would feel intimidated, fearing exposure in the community. After all, he was a successful businessman and a highly regarded citizen of Moab. Perhaps he would even be frightened and willing to do anything. In any case, if the man were agreeable, Bart would borrow the money and promise to repay it. With interest. Of course in this case, Bart would have to expose himself. He couldn't expect the man to loan money without knowing the identity of the borrower.

Bart considered the question of whether he would be able to repay the loan. If he could set up new-identity operations in a few other large cities, he should be able to repay the man in two or three years. And with both fearing exposure, they would guard and protect each other's secret. It seemed like a workable idea.

He needed time to think everything through. There were a lot of ways to get in trouble here. He decided he would call Linda Anderson at the office early. She'd already approved his taking off Monday and Tuesday for the hike. He would ask if he could also take off today. Make it a five-day weekend. He'd tell her he needed an extra day to prepare for the hike.

A happy thought danced in Bart's head. The day he'd be moving into that condo seemed a lot closer now.

20

AFTER A QUICK BREAKFAST at the Rim Rock Diner with Emmett Mitchell, Rivera drove directly to the Health Department. Linda Anderson had just arrived at the office. He skipped the preliminaries.

"Linda, could you check to see if there are death certificates on file for these eleven names?" He handed her a list. "It's very important."

She looked at him over her reading glasses. "Did the deaths take place in Grand County?"

"Yes. They all died on the same day. There was a bus accident on May 26th, 1968. They were children aged six to nine from the old Thompson Springs Orphanage."

"Wouldn't you know it. I gave Bart Winslow the day off. He's our computer guru and knows the vital records system inside out. But I think I can remember how to operate it."

She led him to Bart's workstation behind the office partition and sat down at the terminal. She bowed her head and squinted her eyes for a long moment, as if trying to remember how to operate the system. Then she hit a few tentative keystrokes and waited. The system responded. She typed in the first name on the list, *Harry L. Dixon,* and the date of death. She waited another moment for the system to reply.

"There's no record of his death. Are you sure he died in Grand County?"

"Born and died."

"Let me check for a birth certificate. Do you have the date of birth?"

"He was born on May 6, 1960."

She typed that into the terminal. "Yes. Here it is. We do have his birth record." She looked up at Rivera. "But no death record."

"I'm positive he died in Grand County."

"I only checked our local database. Let me connect with the Office of Vital Records in Salt Lake City and see if they have it in their computer." She turned back to the terminal and typed in the necessary information. In a few seconds, a message was returned to her monitor. She looked at Rivera with a puzzled expression. "No death record up there either."

"Could you check the other ten names?"

"Sure, Manny." She did. The results were the same. Ten birth records and no death records.

"Let me check one more thing, Manny. Our paper records. Maybe the death certificate copies were filed here but the information never found its way into the computer system. All the old paper certificates were supposedly entered into the new system years ago. After that, everything was automated and paperless. Could be these never got entered." She got up from her chair and led Rivera to a locked door. She punched a code into a keypad on the wall. There was a click and she pushed open the door. "This room contains paper copies of the old birth and death certificates. Bart Winslow and I are the only people with the entry pass code to this room." Rivera followed her through the door into a room containing dozens of old filing cabinets.

After some searching, she found the right drawer. She pulled it open, located the death certificate file for the month of May 1968, and paged through the contents. "No, there's no record of any of them here either." She closed the file and looked up at Rivera.

Rivera was now pretty sure what had happened, but he needed to be certain. "Linda, could you check to see if there are death records for the orphanage director and the bus driver? They were also killed in that accident." He pulled out his notepad and flipped through the pages. "The director's name was Eileen Brewster and the driver's name was Curtis Timmons."

Linda reopened the file folder and again paged through the contents. "Yes, there are death certificates for both in here. Let me also check our local database and the database in Salt Lake City." She led Rivera out of the room and back to the computer terminal.

She entered the two names and their date of death into the system. She nodded. "They're both in our local death record database." She tapped some more keys and waited. "And they're both in the state's vital statistics database." She looked up at Rivera.

"Is Bart Winslow the only one who operates this terminal?" asked Rivera.

"Yes. And I'm his backup. We're the only two people who have the access codes."

"And it's been that way since 2005? Just the two of you?"

"Yes. Actually since 2003 when I hired him."

"Let's go back to your office and close the door. I'd like to find out more about Winslow."

Later, back in his office, Rivera sat at his desk reflecting on what he'd learned from Linda about Bart Winslow. He was born and raised in Moab and his computer skills were self taught. He lived in a small cabin behind his parents' house. They were a close-knit family and Bart often went hiking and camping with his father, a former outfitter. As far as Linda knew, Bart had no close friends. Rivera remembered seeing him yesterday when Linda had pointed out the employees who were listed on the 2005 organization chart. He was medium height with a pot belly in the making and a pile of disheveled light-brown hair on his head. His glasses were the old-fashioned kind with heavy black rims. He would never be mistaken for an athlete. Or a model. His face was round and boyish, and there were signs he'd had acne in his youth. His clothing was presentable but unkempt. Rivera remembered how Bart had avoided eye contact with him.

Rivera decided he would intercept Bart and confront him with questions about the death records. There was no proof he was the guilty party but he was certainly a suspect. And even if he were innocent, he should be able to shed some light on how the death records might have been altered.

Rivera picked up the phone and called the Office of Vital Records in Salt Lake City. After talking to the Assistant Director's secretary, then the Assistant Director, and then the Director, he was finally connected with the Chief Systems Analyst. He explained the situation and got to the point.

"Is it possible for a hacker to get into your database and alter the records?"

"No way. There are no links between our system and the public domain. There's no entryway for a hacker to use."

"What about the communications links to the District Health Department offices like the one we have here in Moab?"

"There are links to each of the district offices, but those links are encrypted and access-code protected."

"So someone working in a local health department could access your computer."

"Only if they have the correct access code. And when they do access our system, all they can do is fill out their portion of new birth and death record forms. They can't alter anything previously stored in the system."

"Suppose someone in a district office who had the proper access code was a hacker. Could he find a way to make changes to your records?"

There was a pause. "Well, first of all, anyone issued the code has to be bonded. So they can't have a police record or anything like that. We assume they're good guys. Could they make changes if they decided to go rogue?" Another pause. "No, I doubt it. The database portion of the system is password protected. Only two of us up here in Salt Lake City can access it."

"Suppose he was a really talented hacker. Let's say world class."

"You know, I helped set up this system years ago. And I've enhanced its security several times over the years. I have high confidence a hacker couldn't get through. I don't know of a way to do it. Is it possible? I'm not world class so I guess I'd have to say … it wouldn't be impossible. But it's highly unlikely."

Rivera thanked the man for his help and promised to call back if there were any further developments. Now he wondered if Bart was capable of hacking into the password-protected portion of the vital records system. It sounded like it would be extremely difficult.

According to Linda Anderson, he barely finished high school. But she did say he was a whiz with computers. Rivera needed to talk to Winslow as soon as possible. But he recognized a fundamental problem. If Winslow was the one who had done the hacking, he could simply deny it. Then what would Rivera do? How could he ever prove who altered the records? He had no idea.

21

RIVERA RANG THE DOORBELL of the Winslow residence and waited. He looked at his watch. The morning was half gone. A man wearing threadbare jeans, a rust-colored T-shirt, and sandals answered the door. He was Rivera's height with a lean athletic build and grey hair. Rivera estimated his age to be late fifties. The deputy introduced himself and asked if Bart was at home.

"I don't think so. I'm his father. I believe he's at work," said Mr. Winslow.

"No. He's not there. Linda Anderson said he called in this morning and asked for the day off. She said he needed to do some things to get ready for a hike tomorrow. I'd like to ask him a few questions related to an investigation I'm conducting."

Mr. Winslow looked puzzled. "I don't understand why he needed to take today off. I've already made all the preparations for the hike. Tomorrow we're leaving for a four-day exploration of Robbers Roost Canyon." He paused, as if trying to understand the situation.

"Bart lives in the cabin behind our house. His truck's not here so I doubt he's at home, but let's go check anyway."

He led Rivera through the house down a long hallway and out the back door. They walked across a grassless backyard under a pair of cottonwood trees to the cabin. Mr. Winslow knocked. No answer. He reached into his pocket and retrieved a set of keys on a ring. He unlocked the door and pushed it open. They stepped inside.

"Nope. No one home," said Mr. Winslow. "Is there anything else I could help you with?"

"Any idea where I might find him?"

"Let's go back to the house and talk. I'll try to think of all the places he might have gone."

They returned to the house and entered an office. Winslow sat down behind a desk and invited Rivera to have a seat in a leather chair. Rivera surveyed the room. It was a backcountry aficionado's dream. One wall was covered with topographic maps and aerial photographs. Another wall was filled with framed photographs of mountains, arches, rivers, sunsets, natural bridges, and hikers on trails. A flat file with eight drawers sat in the corner of the room, an open drawer revealing a thick stack of topo maps. A gun case contained a collection of hunting rifles and scopes. Stuffed heads of elk, mule deer, and desert bighorn sheep stared down at Rivera. A police scanner squawked periodically from the corner of the room. On a shelf behind the desk were an intercom unit and a collection of geodes and petrified wood. A framed photograph of a handsome young man in an Army uniform was prominent on the desk.

Winslow must have noticed Rivera staring at the photograph. "That's a picture of my son Jack. He was Bart's older brother by two years. He was killed three years ago in Iraq by a damned IED." Winslow's eyes wandered. "I wish he'd never have joined up. I tried to talk him out of it, but he felt he had a duty to his country. He was like that. An amazing young man. And smart. I mean straight A's in high school and the University of Utah. Quarterback of his high-school football team. Hollywood good looks and very popular with the girls. He had it all. After Jack died, things were never the same around here."

Rivera shifted in his chair. "I'm sorry." There was a long period of uncomfortable silence.

"Thankfully, we still have Bart," Winslow finally managed.

Rivera glanced around the room. "I see you're a lover of the backcountry."

A hint of a smile came to Winslow's face. He nodded. "I spent most of my life exploring the Four Corners region. I haven't seen all of it, no one has, but I've seen a lot of it. Mountains, rivers, mesas, canyons, you name it. I used to be in the outfitting business. I'm retired now, but I still like to explore. I go into the backcountry nearly every week. When Jack left home and joined the Army, Bart became my main hiking partner. This intercom here is connected to his cabin. We use it a lot. It's like he lives with us but still has his privacy. We enjoy each other's company and we spend a lot of time exploring remote places. Preferably places where few people have ever been."

"What's the police scanner for?"

He laughed. "Nearly everyone I know has one. Moab's a small town. We don't have a twenty-four-hour news station to keep us up-to-date on the local goings-on. The scanner is like having a CNN channel dedicated exclusively to Moab. If something important is happening, it usually involves the police. Those of us with scanners learn about it right away. I'm a Search-and-Rescue volunteer so it comes in handy there too. If someone in the backcountry needs help, all of us SAR types learn about it quickly and can react sooner."

Rivera nodded. "Good idea."

"You asked me where Bart might be. If he's not at work, the only thing I can suggest is that he's decided the packing list I made for our hike is missing something he wants. I've got all the gear we'll ever need so I'm guessing it must be about food. I usually pack energy bars and packets of freeze dried food for our meals. It keeps the weight of our packs down. The packets of freeze dried food make pretty good meals when added to boiling water, but Bart doesn't particularly agree with that notion. My guess is he went to City Market for hamburger meat, cheese, buns, cookies, and so forth. And if not City Market, then one of the smaller grocery stores."

Rivera stood up. "I'll start looking there. What kind of vehicle does he drive?"

"It's a 1986 Ford pickup, dark brown and beat-up."

"Thanks very much for your help, Mr. Winslow. When Bart returns home, would you please give me a call and let me know?"

"Will do. And please call me Henry. It's been a real pleasure meeting you."

Rivera gave him a business card listing his phone numbers. They shook hands and he left, heading for Skip Kennison's real estate office.

Rivera thought about Henry Winslow as he drove. He liked him. He seemed like a man who knew what he wanted to do in life and did it. He was personable and interesting. His relationship with Bart seemed special. They were obviously very close. Rivera found himself wondering if Bart, the product of a good family, could really have had anything to do with felonious computer hacking.

Rivera pulled to the curb in front of Kennison Real Estate. He entered the small stucco building and asked the receptionist for Mr. Kennison. He learned Kennison was working today at the MountainView subdivision and wasn't expected back in the office until late in the day. Rivera was familiar with the new subdivision. It was located in San Juan County just over the county line.

Fifteen minutes later, Rivera turned into the MountainView subdivision and slowly drove the gentle curves of a new asphalt road. Half-a-dozen south-west-style houses had been completed and appeared occupied. Several others were in various stages of construction. He spotted a trailer with a sign out front that read *Kennison Real Estate, Lots for Sale*. He parked in the gravel parking lot in front of the trailer and entered.

The office was small and minimally furnished with a desk, a drafting table, two filing cabinets, and a small refrigerator. The walls were covered with subdivision plats, house floor plans, and aerial photographs. Kennison was just hanging up the phone.

"Hi. Come on in," said Kennison with a salesman's smile as he stood up and approached Rivera.

"Good morning, Mr. Kennison." Rivera introduced himself as they shook hands. "I'm here on business. I'd like to ask you a few questions about an investigation I'm conducting."

Kennison seemed surprised. His smile faded. "Well...sure. Please have a seat."

After some small talk about the subdivision and the Moab economy, Rivera took out his notepad and got to the point.

"I'm investigating the February Flanagan murder. There were some files in the trunk of his car. One of them contained an article from the *Times-Independent* about your wedding. Can you think of any reason why he'd have an interest in you?"

The pertinent questions and their answers were pretty much the same as the interview.Rivera had conducted with Kennison's best man. Kennison knew who Flanagan was but said they had never met or spoken with one another. He had no idea why Flanagan had been interested in him or his wife. "Kind of creepy," Kennison had said.

As Rivera pushed open the door of the Sheriff's Department building, Millie Ives motioned him over to her dispatcher's workstation.

"There are two County Councilmen in Sheriff Bradshaw's office right now," she said in a whisper. "I heard raised voices so I don't think it's a pleasant meeting. And I heard a rumor last night that Denny Campbell has decided to run for sheriff next year. He's telling his friends that capital crime in Moab is out of control. He says he doesn't think Sheriff Bradshaw is up to the job anymore."

Rivera nodded in appreciation of the heads-up, went to his office, and closed the door. He checked his desk for a pink message slip telling him that Bart's father had called. Found none. Earlier, Rivera had driven all over Moab, walked through the grocery stores, and checked the parking lots of the camping supply stores, but was unable to turn up any sign of Bart. Of course, he could have passed within a block of Bart driving on another street and not seen him. The best strategy now seemed to be waiting for Mr. Winslow's phone call telling him that Bart had returned home.

The waiting was difficult, especially knowing what was currently taking place in Bradshaw's office. The pressure from the council members on the Sheriff was ratcheting higher with each passing day. Jill Bradshaw and her husband were very close. Her cancer had to weigh heavily on his mind every minute of every hour. There was a single moment yesterday when Rivera glanced at Bradshaw sitting in his office just staring out into space with a defeated look on his face. He must have been dreading the inevitable and feeling the frustration of not being able to do anything about it. Bradshaw was a highly competent man, a top-notch problem solver. But Jill's problem was outside his sphere of competence. Despite Bradshaw's monumental personal problem, Rivera had never heard him complain.

Rivera checked his watch again. It was ten-fifteen in the morning. He'd made a lot of progress uncovering the false identity business, but he still had no suspect for the killings. He urgently wanted to break the case and reduce the pressure on his boss but could think of nothing to do but sit there, helplessly waiting for a phone call from Henry Winslow.

22

IT WAS ALMOST NOON. Bart Winslow waited on the sidewalk, looking for an opening in the flow of traffic so he could cross Main Street. He watched as a new dark-green Jeep Rubicon with an open top cruised by. It had big tires and a jacked-up suspension, just like what he wanted. The tan bare-chested young man driving the vehicle was talking over the loud music to a laughing blonde wearing white shorts and a tank top. Bart stood there, watching them until they were out of sight.

He crossed the street and walked toward the Moab Information Center, a large Chamber of Commerce facility in the center of town which provided brochures, maps, souvenirs, books, and hiking-trail information to out-of-town visitors. He picked up one of the public telephones just outside the building. He was nervous but after thinking everything through, he'd decided the best approach was a direct one.

Earlier in the morning, he'd driven into town and parked his pickup in the small lot behind the Red Rock Bakery and Café. He'd entered the café through the rear door, ordered coffee and a sweet roll, and sat there, carefully reviewing his options and the possible consequences of each. Several cups of coffee later, he decided he clearly had the upper hand. The man would most likely be cooperative rather than jeopardize the fine life he now enjoyed in Moab. Bart also concluded honesty would be the best policy. Just tell everything like it is.

He took a deep breath and let it out. Dialed the number. A man answered on the first ring and identified himself.

"Can I help you?" He had a self-confident voice.

"You're going to think this is a very odd phone call."

"What? Who is this?"

"I'll remain anonymous for the time being. But you'll want to hear what I'm about to say."

"What do you mean? Who is this?"

"I know you're not who you say you are. And I have proof."

There was a long pause. "You're not making any sense. What is it you want?" The voice now sounded less confident.

"I have it on good authority that you purchased a false identity from a guy in New Jersey."

Another long pause. He could hear the man breathing. "I don't like anonymous phone calls. Maybe we should get together and talk about this face-to-face like gentlemen."

"I mean you no harm. And this is not an extortion call. My purpose is to propose a business deal to you. If you say no, then that's the end of it."

"What did you have in mind?"

The man sounded apprehensive. That was a good sign. "I would like to borrow fifty thousand dollars from you. I would repay you within three years. At a suitable interest rate of course."

"If I loan you the money, how do I know that would be the end of it? That you wouldn't come back and ask for more?"

"Because that's all I need. I'm a long-time resident of Moab. And I'm a man of my word."

"That's all you *need?*" There was a nervous laugh. "What do you need it for?"

"I'd like to make a down payment on a condo and buy a new Jeep."

"I see." Another pause. "How do I know you'll be able to make the payments on the condo and the Jeep? What if you go bankrupt and can't repay me?"

Bart liked the way the conversation was going. The man sounded like he was considering the proposition. "I have a job. I'm a systems analyst. I'm quite sure I can make the payments."

There was a long period of silence, as though the man was processing what Bart had told him. "What was your role in producing my new identity?"

Bart hesitated. "I didn't say I had a role. Only that I'd heard about it."

"Listen, I think we'd better be completely honest with each other. If I can't believe what you're telling me, how can I trust you with a loan?"

"Okay, I see what you mean. I guess you're right. I work in the District Health Department office here in Moab. I came up with the idea for the new identities and implemented the whole thing. My cousin Ralph Winslow in Newark is my partner. He does the marketing." Bart found it easy to talk to the man. He seemed reasonable and intelligent. It was almost as though he'd found a new partner.

"Ralph was recommended to me by some of my associates in New York. I thought the whole idea was his. I didn't know he had a partner. So you're the brains behind the operation." The man sounded like he was smiling at his new discovery.

"That's correct. I figured out the whole thing and set it up." Bart enjoyed the opportunity for a little braggadocio.

"Well, the new identity business is a great idea. You helped me restart my life. And I appreciate it. But with your job and this extra income on the side, I'd have guessed you'd have plenty of money for down payments and such."

"The job doesn't pay much. And Ralph is a bit of a slacker. We haven't sold many identities. One or two a year is all. I'm thinking of expanding into other cities."

"OK. Listen, you sound like a reasonable sort of fellow. I think I might be able to help you. But this has to remain between you and me. For obvious reasons."

"Yes, of course." Bart's spirits soared but he forced himself to remain calm and business-like.

"There'll be no paperwork on this," the man said. "Just two men giving their word to one another."

"Right."

"And all transactions will be in cash."

"Sure. No problem."

"You'll have three years to pay me back. Interest will accrue at six percent per annum. One final payment of principal and interest. Is that acceptable?"

"Yes. Thank you very much. I won't disappoint you."

"I don't want to transfer the money to you in the middle of Moab. Too many curious eyes. I have a ranch down in Summit Point. I'll give it to you there. You know where Summit Point is?"

"Sure. Down in San Juan County."

"Good. The front gate is 2.2 miles south of the village on the east side of Ucolo Road. You can't miss it. There's a large gold star welded onto the gate. I'll leave the gate unlocked. Drive on in but be sure to close it behind you so the cattle don't wander out. I'll be waiting for you at the ranch house. Let's say this evening at six o'clock. I'll have the cash ready for you."

"I'll be there."

"And not a word of this to anyone. Needless to say, I'm more than a little nervous about all this. I have a good life here and I don't want it destroyed."

"This will be just between the two of us."

"Good. Of course, I've got you over a barrel too. If I go down, you go down with me. And so does your cousin Ralph."

"I understand perfectly. There won't be any problems. I'll see you at six." He hung up.

Bart was elated as he trotted across Main Street and returned to his pickup truck. He felt like jumping up and letting out a cheer. His whole life was about to change. He decided to drive over to the condos, tour them once again, and make an appointment with the real estate agent. Then he'd drive over to the Jeep dealership and kick a few tires.

23

RIVERA REACHED FOR THE phone on his desk and picked it up. He began dialing the number for the Winslow residence, then stopped. He dropped the phone back into its cradle. He was letting his impatience get the better of him. Henry Winslow said he'd call when Bart came home, and Rivera judged him to be a man of his word.

So if Bart wasn't home, where the heck was he? Had something happened to him?

Rivera considered Bart. He seemed like a gentle person, nerdy and introverted. Was it possible he was the perpetrator of the false identity operation? It didn't seem likely, but suppose he was. Suppose he really did have the capability to hack through the firewall of the Office of Vital Statistics system in Salt Lake City. Then how did he go about selling new identities to the criminals McKelvey had told him about? Bart didn't seem the type who would have those kinds of connections or know how to deal with people like that. And where was the profit from the identity sales? A quick check of

Bart's local bank records had shown modest balances in his checking and savings accounts. He lived at home in a small cabin and drove an old pickup. This line of thought seemed to be unproductive.

Rivera took his thinking to the next level. Suppose Bart was not as gentle as he seemed. Suppose he was fully capable of computer hacking, that he'd created the false identities, and that he'd somehow found a way to handle the marketing. Perhaps with a partner. Suppose also that he was much wealthier than he let on and that he had significant funds stashed in an out-of-state bank or an offshore account. Then suppose that February Flanagan, as a result of his probing into county activities, had gotten onto Bart's little scheme. The files found in his car certainly suggested he had. If all that were true, was it possible Bart had somehow discovered Flanagan was getting close? After all, Bart was in the office during Flanagan's many visits with Linda Anderson. He would have known Flanagan was asking a lot of questions, some of them most likely about the Health Department's responsibilities in the vital statistics area. Is it possible then, that Bart killed February to protect himself? The question hung in Rivera's mind. Bart didn't seem like a killer, but it was certainly possible. And if Bart himself wasn't the killer, maybe he had an associate who was.

Although fraught with assumptions, Rivera continued down this trail of logic. If Bart did kill Flanagan, then why was Reynolds killed? He'd been showing pictures around town, but he claimed they were people from New York who might have had a revenge motive for killing Flanagan. That didn't seem to pose a threat to Bart in any way. So Bart would have absolutely no reason to kill Reynolds.

Rivera tumbled those thoughts around in his brain, testing them for reasonableness, looking for flaws. Then he rejected the whole idea. Flanagan and Reynolds were killed with the same gun, and most assuredly by the same person. If Bart had had no reason to kill Reynolds, then he hadn't killed Flanagan either. Another dead end.

The puzzle wasn't coming together. Rivera took another tack. He tried looking at the whole sequence of events through Flanagan's eyes. How did Flanagan get on to Bart's illegal operation in the first place? What was his first clue? Maybe he was investigating something else related to vital statistics and that led to his uncovering Bart's operation. Rivera picked up the phone and dialed Linda's number.

"Hi, Linda. Just a couple of more questions."

"Oh, you're lucky you caught me, Manny. I was just on my way out the door for a long weekend at Yellowstone. How can I help you?"

"During Flanagan's visits to your office, did he ever ask about birth certificates or death certificates or any subject related to the Office of Vital Statistics?"

"Sure. He delved into everything we do, including our role in originating and transmitting vital statistics information to Salt Lake City."

"Did he ever interview Bart Winslow?"

"No, absolutely not. I was the only one he talked to. I insisted on that because I didn't want him bothering my people. They had too much work to do."

"OK, Linda, thanks. Have fun at Yellowstone." He hung up.

So the question remained. What exactly was the original trigger that started Flanagan's investigation? It was a question for which Rivera could supply no answer. There was also an important corollary question. How did the killer learn that Flanagan had become a threat to him? Rivera had no answer for that either.

He sat back in his chair, took a deep breath, and exhaled. There was something else in the back of his mind that had been troubling him. What if there was absolutely no connection between Flanagan's murder and Bart's false identity business? What if Flanagan was murdered for some totally unrelated reason? That was looking more and more like a real possibility. Rivera had been connecting the two crimes solely on the basis of the files he'd found in the trunk of Flanagan's car. If that was wrong, then he'd completely wandered off the main trail of logic. Way off.

If there was no connection, then Flanagan and Reynolds had likely been killed for reasons related to events in New York. That had to be correct. But there also had to be some kind of Moab-New York connection. Since Reynolds was killed in Moab, someone locally must have felt threatened by the pictures he was showing around town.

Were Flanagan's murder and Bart's new-identity operation linked or not? That was the key question. Rivera decided to proceed under the assumption they were, at least until he had reason to believe otherwise. It seemed the only sensible course of action, based upon what he now knew. He also reminded himself that he hadn't yet proven Bart masterminded the false identities.

He looked at his watch. It was eleven-thirty and still no word from Henry Winslow.

As Rivera sat and waited, Bradshaw's counsel kept echoing in his brain. *Take a larger view.* He decided to go through everything in the case file one more time since he had nothing better to do.

He spread all the material from the case file across his desk. He started by reading everything in Flanagan's five files. Then he reviewed the crime scene reports from Flanagan's murder site at Labyrinth canyon and Reynolds's motel room. He noticed nothing new in any of them. He practically had them memorized by now. Next came the autopsy reports. Then the personal effects list. Nothing resonated. He reread his own notebook, reviewing the interviews he'd had with persons connected to the case. Nothing he read caused him to challenge any of his current ideas or suggested new lines of thought. The final items in the case file were the two photographs of Flanagan that Cosgrove had given him. He glanced at them and dropped them on top of the pile of papers he'd just reviewed. Nothing left to review.

He sat back and stared at the wall. Waiting around was not something he did well. He picked up the photograph of Flanagan sitting in his office and looked at it again. Flanagan looked like someone he would have enjoyed getting to know. He had an interesting face. In a way, they were in the same business. Ridding society of the criminal element. Making the world a better place to live in. He was about to toss the photograph back on his desk when something caught his eye. Resting on the shelf over Flanagan's desk were three Navajo kachinas, two Indian pots, and three bronze shaman figures. Having recently become familiar with Cosgrove's bronzes, he now realized that all three shamans were Cosgrove's. He recognized one of them as Moab Man, as it had one arm up and one down. But seeing them now in the photograph and realizing he hadn't recognized them as Cosgrove's when he first saw them in Flanagan's office, he wondered what else he hadn't noticed during that first visit. He decided to return to Flanagan's office and take another look at everything, this time with a more educated eye. It might be a waste of time but at the moment he had nothing better to do.

He called the Benson residence and talked to Claudia.

"Ms. Benson, I'm sorry to bother you again but I'd like to take another look at February's office."

"Of course, Deputy Rivera. Come on over."

He rang the doorbell and listened to the now-familiar chimes. Claudia's tabby cat was in her arms when she opened the door.

"How nice to see you again, Deputy. Come right in. You know where the office is."

"Thank you. I'll only be a minute."

He entered the office and surveyed it. Looked at everything carefully. Things seemed exactly as they had been the first time he visited. The same items on the desk, the same newspapers and magazines, the same dust. There was nothing that suggested a new line of thought. He held up the photograph of Flanagan sitting at his desk and compared it to the actual office. Everything matched perfectly except for the items on the shelf above the desk. The Moab Man shaman in the photograph was missing. He wondered if perhaps Claudia had removed it and placed it somewhere else in the house. He also wondered if whoever took the hard drive had snatched one of the bronzes.

Of course, there was still no proof the person who had broken into the office had also murdered Flanagan.

Only conjecture. But if the theory was correct, the killer might be in possession of one of Cosgrove's Moab Man sculptures. Rivera wondered how many of that model Cosgrove had made. Meriwether Williams had one in his collection. How many others were there? And who had them? There were probably many since Moab Man was a very popular petroglyph in the area. But what if Cosgrove had made only a few? If Rivera could somehow track them all down, it might narrow down the field of suspects.

He walked into the kitchen and asked Claudia if she'd removed one of the shaman bronzes from the office. She said no, she hadn't paid much attention to them. Then she presented a warm paper bag to Rivera. He opened it and peeked inside. He smiled, said thank you, and left.

Rivera looked expectantly at Meredith as he entered the Sheriff's Department. She was shaking her head.

"No calls?"

"No calls."

Rivera's stomach was as reliable as a factory whistle. It began rumbling at exactly noon each day. He left the office and drove down Main Street to Wendy's. He wolfed down a cheeseburger and an order of fries, then drove over to Cosgrove's studio to ask him about the shaman sculptures.

"I produced molds for ten different bronzes, each one patterned after a different shaman petroglyph found on canyon walls in the Four Corners area," said Cosgrove. "I've cast and sold many of each type. Maybe three dozen apiece. They're pretty popular. Some of my clients have a complete set of ten. It seems having the whole set has become a sort of high-desert status symbol." He chuckled and shrugged.

Rivera felt deflated. Nothing seemed to be going his way. "I was hoping there would only be a few of each and that you could tell me where all the Moab Man bronzes were located. I'll admit it was a long shot."

Cosgrove raised his eyebrows. "Moab Man? Well, Manny, there was only *one* of those. I made it as a special gift for February Flanagan. It was a kind of celebration of our friendship."

"Are you positive there's only one?"

"Absolutely. I destroyed the mold after I cast the first one. When I presented the sculpture to Feb, I told him he was one of a kind, just like the Moab Man petroglyph and the bronze I cast in its image."

24

AS HE DROVE HIS PICKUP back to the office, Rivera's mind was racing. He was processing the information he'd just received from Cosgrove, his orderly mind trying to fit a new fact into his understanding of the case. There was only one Moab Man bronze in existence and Meriwether Williams had it in his office. Could he be the one who stole it from February Flanagan's office? Was he the one who took Flanagan's hard drive?

Rivera worked hard at suppressing his tendency of jumping to conclusions. And right now, he had to work especially hard. Williams was an important citizen of Moab and Sheriff Bradshaw wouldn't appreciate it if Rivera made an accusation that proved to be false. Things like that didn't go over very well in a small town. Williams, a known collector of Cosgrove bronze shamans, could have come by the Moab Man shaman in any number of ways. He could have received it as a gift or he might have picked it up at a flea market or garage sale.

Rivera considered a new question. If Williams did steal the shaman, was it possible he also killed Flanagan? As soon as he asked the question, he knew the answer. Williams was crippled. There was no way he could have carried Flanagan's body from the two-track road to the place where the corpse was found. Could he have dragged him? Possibly. But he wouldn't have been able to gather the heavy rocks that hid Flanagan's body, much less carry them uphill.

Rivera decided to take the most straightforward approach. He would revisit Williams at his office and just ask him where he got the shaman. Most likely he'd have a rational explanation. Then perhaps Rivera could backward trace the travel of the bronze from Williams to Flanagan's office, and in the process identify the person who stole it. He reminded himself not to get irreversibly locked into the idea that it had been stolen. It was still possible, for example, that one of Claudia Benson's grandkids had removed it from the office without her knowledge. From there it could have gone anywhere.

Before driving over to the Uranium Building to re-interview Williams, Rivera decided to run a routine check on him for wants and warrants. He returned to his office and typed Williams's name and home-town into his computer. The system returned a nega-tive response. But his date of birth caught Rivera's eye. It was April 15, 1962. The date struck a chord in his memory. Not because it was income tax day, but because he had seen it somewhere else. Recently. Then he remembered. He took out his notepad and flipped through the pages until he got to the list of names he'd copied from the gravestones in the Thompson Springs Cemetery. There it was. Richard Williams, born April 15, 1962. Was it just a coincidence? They had the same last name and the same date of birth. To double check, he connected with the Utah Department of Motor Vehicles database. The name on his driver's license was R. Meriwether Williams.

Coincidences were piling up fast. Rivera sat back in his chair and considered the implications. The Moab Man bronze, the date of birth, and now the name, at least partially. There had to be something to all of this. But he needed to proceed carefully. A mistake could prove embarrassing to the sheriff at a time when he could least afford it. Rivera had seen no middle initials on the homemade gravestones at the cemetery. Linda Anderson had told him there was a copy of Richard Williams's birth certificate in her records. Just as there was for each of the other ten orphans. But he'd never actually looked at them. Now he needed to know if there was a middle name or initial on the Williams birth certificate.

Unfortunately, there was no way to determine that detail. Linda Anderson was on the road to Yellowstone and Bart Winslow was nowhere to be found. They were the only ones with the access codes to the computer system and the paper records room. Rivera felt himself becoming frustrated again. He picked up the phone and called the Chief Systems Analyst at the Office of Vital Records.

"Hello again, Deputy. How can I help you?"

"I need to check a birth certificate. The Health Department Director and her systems analyst here in Moab are both unavailable. Could you help me? It's urgent."

"Be glad to. What do you need?"

Rivera explained what he was looking for.

"Can do," said the analyst, "But I'll have to get back to you later."

"It's really urgent. Is there any way someone could help me right now?"

"No, our system will be down for about eight more hours. Our computer vendor and a security expert are in here right now upgrading the system's security software. It turns out you were right. After our conversation this morning about hacking, I got worried. I checked the system access files and found some anomalies, so I had to take action right away. We can't take a chance with someone altering important records. I shut down the system and called in the experts. It looks like someone has been monkeying with the death record database. We haven't figured out yet exactly what was done but we're working on it."

Rivera left his phone numbers and asked the man to call him as soon as he was able to check Williams's birth record.

Rivera slammed his fist on his desk. Against his better judgment, he picked up the phone and called Henry Winslow next to see if his son had returned home. He hadn't. Winslow reassured Rivera he'd call him just as soon as Bart arrived home. Now Rivera was stuck. And he didn't like sitting around and waiting. He had to get an answer to the middle-initial question before he approached Williams. If only the volunteer in Thompson Springs had put middle initials on the gravestones.

That thought suggested an idea. He left the office, jumped into his pickup, and headed toward Thompson Springs. At least driving made him feel like he was doing something.

He drove fast and arrived at Thompson Springs in thirty-five minutes. At the cemetery, he turned into the gravel driveway and skidded to a halt. Steve was hoeing weeds in front of a grey monument. He looked in Rivera's direction, pushed his glasses higher on his nose with his index finger, and squinted. Then he smiled.

Rivera trotted over to him. "Steve, when you managed the cemetery, did you keep records of all the burials?"

"Sure did."

"Do you still have them?"

"Sure do. They're in the office file cabinets."

"I'm trying to find out the middle name or initial of one of the orphans killed in the bus accident. It wasn't on the grave marker."

"Let's go over to the office and take a look at the files."

Steve hobbled toward the stone building. Rivera followed.

"I rarely go in here anymore," said Steve as his shaky sun-blotched hand selected a key from his key ring. After a few errant stabs at the lock, he managed to insert the key. He twisted it and pulled open the door.

They stepped into the warm stale air. The room was dark except for shafts of light coming through the doorway and a small window covered with bars. Steve glanced around the office. "Being in here brings back lots of memories." He walked past a dust covered desk to a bank of filing cabinets. "The burial plot forms are filed alphabetically. What name are you interested in?"

"Richard Williams." Rivera unclipped a flashlight from his belt and assisted Steve's search with a beam of light.

Steve adjusted his bifocals and read the labels on the file drawers. "It should be in this drawer." He pulled it open and fingered through the file folders. "Here it is." He extracted a single sheet of paper and scanned it. He shook his head and handed it to Rivera.

Rivera studied the form. "No middle name or initial. Damn. I wasted a trip." Irritated by his run of bad luck, he stepped outside into the fresh air. He pushed his hat back, wiped his forehead with his sleeve, and waited for Steve to lock up.

Steve stuck his head through the open doorway. "Hold on a second, Deputy. Do you remember the story I told you about Ollie threatening to burn down the abandoned orphanage because it was a constant reminder of the day the bus went off the cliff and killed all those kids?"

"Yes, I do."

"Well, he never did burn it down. Came to his senses, I guess. But at the time, he sounded serious. I figured he just might do it. So I went into the orphanage building one afternoon and removed everything of value. I stored the stuff in the back room here. One of the things I rescued was the orphanage files. Maybe his full name is in there."

Rivera felt a stir of excitement. Maybe his luck was about to change.

They went into the back room. After twenty minutes of sweating and searching through cardboard boxes, Rivera pulled out a folder with the name *Williams* on the tab. He opened it and directed the flashlight beam onto the papers. There he found the full name: *Richard Meriwether Williams.*

Rivera now had exactly what he needed. He thanked Steve profusely.

"Glad to be of service," said Steve with a self-satisfied smile.

Rivera took the orphanage file folder and the cemetery record with him when he left. As he sped back to Moab, he sorted through the facts and began putting the pieces of the puzzle together. It began with someone deleting the death records of the orphans killed in the bus accident. The names were then used to create false identities. Maybe that someone was Bart Winslow, maybe someone else. Too soon to be sure. In any case, the identities were sold to individuals who used them for various illicit purposes. According to what Frank McKelvey had learned, two had been used in insurance scams, two were purchased by illegal immigrants, and one was acquired by a criminal evading arrest by the police. There were eleven orphans so six names were unaccounted for. And now another had been identified. It was curious this one had ended up living in Moab.

Rivera wondered what Richard Meriwether Williams's real name was and why he'd acquired a false identity. What was he hiding from? Had he done something illegal or had he simply decided to start life over and leave the past behind? Rivera exited I-70 and turned south on U.S. 191 toward Moab. One thing was certain—all five of February's files were related to a single investigation he'd been conducting. And the wedding article from the *Times-Independent* was there not because it involved Kennison but because it contained a photograph of Williams, his best man.

Williams was considered a pillar of the Moab community, but suppose his history was actually one of crime. Suppose further that he'd bought a new identity and settled in Moab. Perhaps he saw Grand County, Utah on his birth certificate, became curious about the place where he was "born," and decided to check it out. Maybe he liked the area and stayed. Then suppose Flanagan had seen him in town and recognized him from his previous life. Maybe that was what launched Flanagan on his investigation. It was probably around the time Claudia recognized a change in her husband, when he became distant and preoccupied. That would make sense. Then as Flanagan dug deeper into the story, he must have somehow connected Williams's name and date of birth with the orphans in the bus accident. Perhaps through an internet search. Maybe he'd found the article from the now-defunct Castle Dale newspaper Chris Carey had mentioned. That could have led to a theory about the use of false identities and Flanagan's subsequent telephone call to McKelvey. From there, the trail would have taken Flanagan to the Moab Health Department Office and his interviews with Linda Anderson. Rivera found himself impressed with Flanagan's investigative skills.

Did Williams learn somehow that Flanagan was investigating him and kill him? No, that made no sense. Williams couldn't have carried the rocks used to conceal the body. Maybe an accomplice did it for him.

And how did Reynolds fit into the story? He was showing pictures around town of people who might have had a revenge motive for killing Flanagan. Maybe Williams's photo was in the Reynolds file. Or maybe Williams thought it might be in the file and couldn't take a chance, so he had Reynolds killed.

Cosgrove had said Reynolds's photos looked like they'd been photocopied from newspapers. Maybe they were copied from Flanagan's own newspaper articles. Rivera decided it was time he went through Flanagan's file cabinets and looked at the photographs contained in his collection of newspaper articles.

Rivera descended through the reddish-brown stratum of Moenkopi sandstone on the long downslope into Moab. He crossed the bridge over the Colorado River, now recalling that neither Claudia nor Cosgrove had recognized any of the men in the photos. Surely they would have recognized Williams had his photo been there. But perhaps he had changed his appearance. In any case, Rivera would carefully review Flanagan's archives. He wanted to be absolutely sure about everything before he made a move on Williams.

25

BART WINSLOW WAS KILLING time by driving some of the back roads in the LaSal Mountains and looking at the fall scenery. The air was crisp, the sky was blue, and the aspens were turning golden. The snow at the higher altitudes was melting under the late afternoon sun, and the creeks were running. He drummed his fingers on the steering wheel. Life was good.

His mind was focused on the new condo. After he'd faxed the two new identities to Ralph earlier in the day, he'd met with the real estate agent and toured the condo complex one more time. He'd selected a three-bedroom two-bath unit with a private patio that had a view of the mountains and the Moab Rim. It was perfect. He'd told the agent he would return in the morning to sign a contract and make a down payment. Next week, he would order a brand-new Jeep. He was eager to start his new life.

He looked at his watch. There was still an hour to go before his meeting at the ranch. He hoped his appearance was right. Casual but not too casual. And be sure to speak and act confidently, he reminded himself.

In about thirty minutes, he would descend from the mountains, cross over the pavement of Highway 46, and then take the road south to Summit Point.

Things were finally going his way.

26

RIVERA WALKED UP THE porch steps to the front door of the Benson residence and rang the doorbell. He was smiling when Claudia answered the door.

"You probably think I'm back for more cookies."

She burst into laughter. "Well, I just happen to have some more. Come on in, I'll get you a bagful."

He followed her into the living room. "I'd like to take one more look at February's office. Go through the files."

"Of course." She gestured toward the office. "You know the way."

Rivera entered Flanagan's office and went to the first file cabinet. He pulled open the top drawer and removed the oldest file folder, the one dated 1975. The first newspaper was the May 27th edition of the *New York Times*. He flipped through the front section and found an article on page seven with a February Flanagan byline. The headline read *Union Boss Charged with Extortion*. There were no photographs accompanying the article, so Rivera moved on to the next newspaper.

It was the August 3rd edition of the *Times*. A headline on the front page below the fold read *Councilman Denies Allegations of Kickback Scheme*. The article included a photograph of a young balding councilman with an irate expression. Again, the byline was Flanagan's.

Rivera paged through the newspapers and magazines, scanning Flanagan's articles as fast as he could, pausing only to study any accompanying photographs. He was in a hurry, so he'd developed an efficient system, grasping the next newspaper, paging through it, and scanning for Flanagan's byline. If there were no accompanying photographs, he'd quickly re-file it and move on to the next publication. If the article included photographs, he'd pause and study them, looking for any hint of recognition.

Fifteen minutes into the process, Claudia brought in a small table, set it down next to him, and left. She returned with a tray containing a mug of coffee and a plateful of warm oatmeal-raisin cookies. Boy, could she read his mind. It seemed like he was perpetually hungry. He thanked her and paused to sample the goods. Then he got back to work.

Forty minutes into the process, he came upon a front-page headline story in the *New York Daily News*. The date was November 18, 1996 and the byline belonged to February Flanagan. The headline read *Russian Mafia Operation at Brooklyn Marine Terminal Smashed*. A subheader read *FBI Calls It a Huge Bust*. A sub-sub-header read *Three Elude Capture.* Rivera recognized it as one of the stories William Reynolds had related to him.

Rivera scanned the article. It was much the same as Reynolds had recounted—a major smuggling and hijacking operation conducted by the Russian Mafia. When Rivera turned to page five where the story was continued, he saw photographs of the three men who had escaped and were wanted by the FBI. He stared at one of the faces. It was a man who looked to be in his late twenties with a clean-shaven face and long dark hair. The eyes were unmistakable. It was a young Meriwether Williams without the buzz cut and beard. The name under the photograph was *Boris Petrov.*

27

BORIS PETROV LOOKED AT his watch. His visitor was scheduled to arrive at the ranch house in a few minutes. He was thinking about the phone call he'd made earlier in the day and wondering if the boss was unhappy with him. He remembered every word of the conversation. He replayed it in his mind, listening to the boss's gravelly voice, searching for any sign he was displeased.

"Hi, Boss. It's Boris."

"Well, hello, Boris. It's good to hear from you. How are things in Moab, Utah?"

"Everything is fine. The weather is perfect and the town is full of tourists."

"That's good. And I see our investments are doing well. You're doing a good job and the organization appreciates it. But nowadays we have to move even more cash. Our arrangements with the Mexicans are generating a million a day. Sometimes twice that. We need to find more ways to put the cash to work."

"*I anticipated that. I've just finished setting up accounts in the Caymans. That's where the cash will go first. We fly it in on our own aircraft. The customs guy at the private terminal is now on our payroll. The cash gets deposited in our accounts there in three different banks. Then we quickly transfer it to our accounts in Switzerland. From there it's transferred again to London where our new investment companies put it to work in Europe and America. The investment companies are all shells with no employees and the investment decisions are all made by me.*"

"*Good job.*"

"*Yes, sir, all is going well on that front. But I do have a small problem.*"

"*What's that?*"

"*I need the services of Dimitri again.*"

"*Again? This is the third time. What is it now?*"

"*It couldn't be helped. Do you remember that guy in Newark who sold me a new identity? His name is Ralph Winslow. Well, it turns out he has a partner right here in Moab who's the brains of the operation. Somehow the Moab partner made the connection and is now hitting me up for a loan.*"

"*How did you handle it?*"

"*I told him I'd loan him fifty grand for three years. He's coming to the Summit Point ranch tonight to pick it up. That's why I need Dimitri.*"

"*You're bringing a lot of attention to yourself, Boris. We need you to manage our investments, not go to the federal pen.*"

"*Yes, sir.*"

"Don't get me wrong. We think you're doing a great job. We just need you to stay out of the limelight. Dimitri is somewhere in Farmington now. He just finished a job for us there. I'll route him up to your ranch. What time is the problem arriving?"

"He's supposed to be there at six o'clock."

"Okay. Consider it done. We'll take care of the Newark partner too."

"I'll also need Dimitri to handle the disposal chore."

"I'll tell him. Dimitri is good at his job. He'll enjoy the project."

"He's good but I wish he'd have done a better job disposing of Flanagan's body. I told Dimitri to dig a deep hole someplace remote and bury the body. Instead, he just hid it behind a pile of rocks. That's where all the trouble started."

"Ah, yes, our old friend February Flanagan. He caused us a lot of grief back at the Brooklyn Marine Terminal. Our operation there was a big money maker until he came along and exposed the whole thing. It took us six years to set it up. First we had to infiltrate management. Then the Longshoremen's Union. Then the inspector ranks. Then we had to eliminate key management and union people until we had total control. After that, we made tens of millions each year. It was hugely profitable until Flanagan started his little investigation and ruined the whole thing. Brought the FBI down on us. You were lucky you got away. A lot of our key people went to jail. My brother got twenty to life. I told Dimitri to give Flanagan some extra special treatment before finishing him off. And I

told him to make sure Flanagan understood why. Payback for my brother."

"We had to call Dimitri in on that one. Flanagan spotted me when I was shopping with Claire at the grocery store. He took a long, hard look. I figured my new appearance had probably fooled him. But then, a few months later, I caught him staring at me again in a bookstore. It was then I realized he'd recognized me that first time in the grocery store. So it was either whack him or pull up stakes, establish a new identity, and move somewhere else. I like my life here and that wasn't something I wanted to do."

"I know. We did the right thing with Flanagan. I'm still not sure eliminating the second guy was a good idea but we had to trust your judgment."

"His name was Reynolds. From New York. He was showing pictures around town. I heard they were pictures of people from New York who might have had a score to settle with Flanagan. I couldn't take a chance. My instructions to Dimitri were to finish him and retrieve the pictures. Turns out I was right. My picture was in the folder."

"Which reminds me. If it turns out you have to run someday, you need to make sure you leave no information behind that could compromise our operations."

"I know. I've thought about that. I keep all our information on two laptop computers. And they're always with me."

"Good. You're smart, just like your father was. A chip off the old block. I miss him. We went way back. Two kids growing up on the same block in Smolensk, going to school together, *chasing the girls together. Those were good times. When we came to the United States, we could only find menial jobs. One night, we decided to become partners and establish our own wing of the Russian Mafia. Built it up from west Brooklyn to New York City to the east coast and from there we pushed all the way to the Pacific. Your father was an excellent partner. We still haven't figured out who back shot him or why."*

"He told me lots of stories about you two growing up. He said you were like a brother to him."

"And that makes you my nephew."

"And proud to be."

As Boris reflected on that conversation, he wondered if he was becoming too much of a risk for the organization. Had he become a liability? He wasn't sure. If only February Flanagan hadn't recognized him.

* * *

Bart checked his odometer. At exactly 2.2 miles south of Summit Point village, he saw a steel gate with a decorative gold star. He turned left onto a rutted track, stopped, and got out of the truck. There were no other vehicles traveling on Ucolo Road. All was quiet. He unlatched the gate and pushed it open, the squeaking of the hinges breaking the silence. He drove through and closed the gate per his instructions. He stood there for a long moment and looked around. The ranch was hidden behind a thick mass of juniper trees and scrub oaks. He could see no buildings. The two-track road into the ranch curved to the left and disappeared behind the trees some thirty yards ahead.

He hoisted himself back into the truck, pulled the door closed, and sat there for a long moment. Suddenly he felt a chill run up his spine. He wondered if he was doing a smart thing. This could be dangerous and he hadn't told anyone he was coming here. He thought everything through again, considering the possibilities and measuring the risks. Then he pictured the new condo and Irma sitting with him on the patio. He slid the gearshift lever into drive and rolled forward.

He drove slowly. The road curved back and forth several times, the thicket of trees and brush preventing a clear view forward. Soon he reached a large field with several dozen Herefords grazing on grama grass. At the far end of the clearing was a log ranch house nestled among some cottonwood trees, a maroon barn, and several out-buildings. A pickup was parked in front of the house. Everything looked normal. He felt the tension diminish.

Bart pulled up next to the pickup and got out. He looked at his watch. It was exactly six o'clock. As he walked up the stone pathway to the house, a man appeared at the door. He had a dark beard and supported himself with a cane.

"Hello, Mr. Williams."

The man smiled. "Well, hello. You look familiar but I don't know your name."

"I'm Bart Winslow." He offered his hand and Williams gave him a firm handshake.

"Come on in and let's talk."

They entered a rustic living room with a large stone fireplace and sat down, Bart on the couch, Williams on an overstuffed chair. Williams spoke first. "I've got fifty thousand dollars in cash for you in that satchel over there." He pointed to a blue canvas bag sitting on the dining room table. "But first let's review our agreement. I don't want there to be any misunderstandings. I will loan you fifty thousand dollars cash today at six percent interest per annum compounded. You will pay me the principal and all interest in cash exactly three years from today." He picked up a sheet of paper and glanced at it. "That comes to $59,550.80. Is that agreed to?"

Bart realized he hadn't really thought about how much he'd have to pay Williams when the loan came due. But he figured the guy was in finance so the number should be right. "Yes, that's correct and agreed to."

"And needless to say, not a word of this to anyone. Ever. Understood?"

"Absolutely. My reputation is at risk too," said Bart.

"OK, then we have an agreement. It's all settled. But tell me something. I'm very intrigued by what you've done. How did you come up with the idea for selling new identities? You must be extremely intelligent."

"Well, thank you, sir." Bart looked over at the satchel. He started to get up, then sat back and relaxed. "The whole idea came to me several years ago. I was reading an article in the *Salt Lake Tribune* about how the old concept of orphanages had been replaced with the modern notion of foster homes. The article described several orphanages around the state. One of them was located in Thompson Springs. A sidebar story described a bus accident that took place near there back in the sixties. Eleven children from the Thompson Springs Orphanage were killed. Thompson Springs is located in Grand County and I'm in charge of the vital statistics computer system for the Moab District. So one day, out of curiosity, I took a look at the birth and death records of the kids who were killed. The records were kept in our computer system and the state's computer system. They also existed in paper form in both locations. The idea just hit me. Why not remove the death records, create new identities, and sell them? It seemed like there had to be a market."

Williams glanced at his watch. "I'm not a computer expert, but I'm curious about something. If you could alter the records in both the local and state computers, why didn't you just invent a new name and create a corresponding birth certificate? Wouldn't that be an easier way to produce a new identity you could sell?"

Bart chuckled. "I'm impressed. That's a very insightful question. And the answer is subtlety. The state and county often perform demographic analyses for a wide variety of purposes. Lists of newborns, population trends, county planning, and so forth. There's no predicting what list a newly created name would appear on. And who might notice it. There's also the problem of entering a birth certificate for someone who was born fifty years ago. That's the kind of thing that raises red flags. Altering an old death certificate is something that would likely go unnoticed."

Williams glanced at his watch again. Frowned slightly. "But you also added a college degree to my new identity. And I was able to get an actual transcript from the university. How did that work?"

Bart grinned and leaned forward. He spoke in a conspiratorial tone. "Not only can I hack into the Office of Vital Statistics database in Salt Lake City, I can also hack into most university databases." He explained his technique for substituting a new name on the transcript of a deceased alumnus.

"That's brilliant. Very impressive."

"Thanks." Bart, anxious to get his money and head back to Moab, stood up. "Well, I'd better get going."

"No, no, please sit down and tell me more. I'm intrigued. How did you work out the job history? Mine seemed very authentic."

Bart sat down. It was satisfying to find someone so interested in what he'd done and how he'd done it. Someone he could confide in. He explained to Williams how he listed defunct companies for past work histories. Then he went into detail about how he'd created a virtual company for the current work history and how he provided references on request.

"Ingenious," said Williams. "And you've been able to do all this without anyone catching on?"

"So far, so good. There was a deputy sheriff in the office this week talking to my boss and asking a lot of questions. But I doubt there's a deputy in Utah with the technical know-how to understand what I'm doing. Anyway, I'm told he was investigating the February Flanagan murder, not Bart Winslow's new identity business." He laughed.

Williams laughed without smiling. "Just out of curiosity, what was the deputy's name?"

"Rivera."

"Oh, yeah. I've met him." He glanced at his watch again. "On the phone, you said you're thinking about expanding your operation into other cities. I have contacts in most major cities. I might be able to make some introductions."

"Really? That would be great. Ralph Winslow in Newark is my only partner. He's my cousin. He's pretty slow at finding new clients. I don't think it's a high priority for him. And besides, I'm not sure I trust him. May I ask how much you paid Ralph for your new identity?"

"Sure. I paid him twenty-six thousand dollars."

Bart was stunned. "Well, I was right. He told me he was charging ten thousand." He could feel his face becoming flushed.

Williams laughed. "So he was cheating you."

"You can't trust anyone," said Bart despondently. He heard a vehicle drive up to the ranch house and stop. Then the sound of a vehicle door opening and closing. Then footsteps approaching the door.

"You have a visitor," said Bart as he stood up. "I'd better go now or I'll be late for dinner."

"Just a moment, Bart. I'd like you to meet my associate."

The door opened and a very large man stepped inside. He had greasy brown hair and dark bloodshot eyes that seemed to bulge from his pock-marked face. He said nothing.

"You're late," said Williams, frowning.

The man shrugged.

"Bart, this is Dimitri. He'll take you outside now." Williams looked at Dimitri and nodded.

"Outside? Uh...What about the satchel?" asked a confused Bart. He felt a vise-like grip on his upper arm and then he was being pulled outside.

* * *

Williams remained seated in his chair and waited. Soon he heard the unmistakable snap of Dimitri's handgun and the thump of a body falling to the ground. Dimitri reappeared in the doorway.

"Boris, what you want I do with body," he asked in broken English with a heavy Russian accent.

"Put him in his truck and drive south on Ucolo Road for exactly 7.4 miles. Turn left onto a dirt road that leads to Summit Canyon. Drive in a mile-and-a-half. It's BLM land and no one ever goes back there. Dig a deep hole and bury him in a thicket of junipers. I left you a shovel in the front yard. When you're finished, drive back to the main road. I'll meet you there in exactly two hours. You'll follow me south to the Navajo reservation. We'll leave his pickup there. Then I'll drive you back here. You can hop in your Range Rover and take off."

Dimitri nodded, turned around, and went back outside.

Petrov heard Bart's pickup crank once, then a second time. On the third try, the pickup started. He listened as the hum of the vehicle's engine faded into the distance. He picked up his cell phone, dialed the boss's number, and reported that Dimitri had arrived and the package was being disposed of. Boris wasn't entirely comfortable with the boss's tone of voice.

28

THE SUN HAD DISAPPEARED behind the Moab Rim and dusk was descending on the town as Rivera trotted into the Sheriff's Department building. It was after-hours on a Friday night and he hoped Sheriff Bradshaw would still be in his office. He was. With an ever-thickening case file under his arm, Rivera entered the sheriff's office and closed the door behind him. Bradshaw looked up from the papers on his desk.

"I need to bring you up to date on the Flanagan case. Things are starting to break."

"Have a seat, Manny. What have you got?"

"Someone, I'm assuming it's Bart Winslow, has been selling false identities out of the local Health Department office." Rivera gave Bradshaw the details on how it had been done. "One was sold years ago to a man who has since become a prominent citizen of Moab." Bradshaw's eyebrows went up. "It's Meriwether Williams, the guy who runs Seven Star Investments in the Uranium Building. His complete assumed name is Richard Meriwether Williams, same name as one of the orphans killed in the bus accident back in 1968. The birthdates are identical. Williams's real name is Boris Petrov. He was one of three men who escaped during an FBI bust of a Russian Mafia operation at the Brooklyn Marine Terminal in 1996. February Flanagan broke the case." Rivera placed a copy of the *New York Daily News* on the table and opened it to page five.

Bradshaw looked at the photo of Petrov and nodded. "Sure looks like him. At least a younger version of him." Then he turned to the front page and began reading the story in its entirety. Rivera waited until he finished the article.

"I think we have enough to pick him up" said an anxious Rivera.

Bradshaw paused. "I think before we do anything about picking him up, we'd better notify the FBI since he's their guy. But first of all, how does this tie into the two murders?"

"As best I can figure it, Flanagan must have recognized Petrov here in Moab. On the street, in a store, somewhere. That made him start digging. I figure it was about the time his wife noticed a change in his personality. She said he'd become distant and preoccupied. I think he must have researched Petrov's new name, Meriwether Williams, and found his new date of birth, perhaps through the Bureau of Motor Vehicles like I did. Somehow he found a correlation with the name and birth date of one of the orphans killed in the bus accident. I don't know how he did that. Maybe he found the article in the Castle Dale newspaper that listed the names. The only reason I was able to make the connection was because of the files in Feb's vehicle. Anyway, knowing your guy has assumed someone else's identity makes you dig a lot harder. Keeps you motivated. And Feb was obviously quite brilliant. He visited the cemetery and recorded the names of the eleven orphans and their dates of birth. Then he passed the information to Frank McKelvey, a private eye in New York who was an old friend. McKelvey researched the names and discovered that five of them had been used in false identity schemes. Those cases involved insurance scams, illegal immigrants, and a criminal escaping prosecution. That in turn led Flanagan to his investigation of the Moab Health Department and its role in the vital statistics system, particularly the death records. All aspects of the case were tied together by the five files in the trunk of Flanagan's vehicle."

"Makes sense, but how did Petrov get on to Flanagan?"

"Petrov must have noticed Flanagan looking at him or heard that he was asking questions about him. I don't know for sure," said Rivera.

"So Petrov kills Flanagan and buries him behind a pile of rocks out by Labyrinth Canyon?"

"I don't think so. Petrov is handicapped. I doubt he could have carried those rocks uphill to where

Flanagan's body was found. I think he must have had an accomplice."

"Yeah, some of those rocks looked pretty heavy. And I know for a fact that Williams, er... Petrov, really is handicapped. I've seen him in shorts at the gym. His knee is a mess and there's lots of scar tissue."

"After Petrov had Flanagan killed, he must have snuck into Flanagan's office when Claudia wasn't home, searched the place for incriminating information, and stolen the hard drive. While he was there, he noticed the Cosgrove Moab Man shaman, a sculpture he didn't have in his own collection. He didn't know it was one of a kind. I guess he couldn't resist taking it and adding it to the shaman collection on his office bookshelves. That's eventually what got me on to him."

"So everything was quiet for three years. Everyone figured Flanagan had just skipped town. Then his body is found and a few days later Reynolds shows up in Moab. What then?"

"Reynolds was trying to capitalize on the situation. He'd always wanted to be a successful well-known investigative journalist like Flanagan. He pretended he had helped Flanagan throughout his career in New York. The theory put forth by Sam Enderle, a friend of Flanagan's from New York, was that Reynolds wanted to write a book about the Flanagan/Reynolds collaborative exploits in New York. And being involved in solving Flanagan's murder would add a nice touch to the story. But the truth was that Flanagan had no use for him, no respect at all. So Reynolds shows up here with a sheaf of pictures of people who might have had a revenge motive for killing Flanagan—pictures he'd saved from newspaper articles. Not a bad theory really, and in a way it turned out to be correct. I figure somehow Petrov got wind of the pictures, decided his face might be in one of them, and had Reynolds killed to get the photo file out of circulation."

"And Petrov's beard and buzz-cut fooled those who had looked at the pictures."

"Must have. That and the change in facial characteristics brought on by the passage of time. But to me, the eyes were a dead giveaway."

"OK, Manny. Good job." Bradshaw picked up the telephone, dialed a long-distance number, and asked to speak with Agent Carl Bowers.

"Carl, I'm glad you're still in the office. This is Leroy Bradshaw down in Moab .... Fine. How are things in Salt Lake City? .... Carl, I think we may have someone in our little town that the FBI has been looking for. Name's Boris Petrov, but he's been using the alias Richard Meriwether Williams." Bradshaw sat in silence, jotting down notes, apparently receiving instructions. Then he said "Okay, will do," and hung up the phone.

Bradshaw looked at Rivera. "They want us to do nothing."

29

DIMITRI GLANCED THROUGH THE rear window at the bed of the pickup. One corner of the tarp that covered the body was flapping in the wind. He'd weighted down the edges with rocks from the ranch but one of the rocks had rolled at the last turn in the road. He stopped the vehicle, repositioned the rock, and wedged the shovel across the bed to keep the rock in place. Handling the shovel reminded him of how much he hated digging. When the boss invited him to leave Russia and come to America, Dimitri thought he had laid down his shovel for the last time. He'd hated his job as a ditch digger for the water utility company and swore he'd never again dig another hole. So far, he'd kept that promise to himself. He got back into the vehicle and resumed driving south on Ucolo Road.

Dusk was fast approaching. He leaned forward and squinted, searching for the turnoff. Finally he spotted it, right where Boris said it would be.

Dig a deep hole and bury him. It rankled Dimitri when Boris gave him orders and treated him like he was subservient. Dimitri reported to the boss and no one else. He didn't like Boris and had little respect for him. If he were a real man, he'd have taken care of the exterminations himself. Cleaned up his own mess. He could pull a trigger just as easily as Dimitri could. But no, he claimed he wasn't a killer. Just like his father always did. All brains and no guts. Dimitri wondered what Boris would say if he knew it was Dimitri who killed his father. On the boss's orders. The thought brought a smile to his face. Soon he was laughing out loud.

He turned left onto the rutted dirt road. It wound its way through a thicket of trees. He drove for a mile and a half and brought the vehicle to a stop near the edge of a small canyon. Summit Canyon, he figured. Boris had said it would be on his left.

He got out of the pickup and looked around. All was quiet. There were no buildings or people in sight. He walked to his right and explored an area surrounded by a thick growth of junipers. He selected a spot where the dirt looked soft, then returned to the truck and retrieved the shovel. Out of curiosity, he walked to the edge of the bluff overlooking the canyon and looked down. Two hundred feet below, the bottom was thick with trees and underbrush. He stood there for a moment, his thoughts returning to Boris. Then he hurled the shovel into the canyon. Damned if he was going to dig any more holes. He returned to the pickup, pulled the body out of the bed by its legs, and picked it up. He carried it back to the rim of the bluff, held it out over the edge, and released it. A few seconds later, he heard a loud crack and then a thud. He looked down. It was getting dark but there was still enough light for him to see the body lying on top of a large limb that had been broken off a cottonwood tree by the force of the falling corpse.

Dimitri drove the pickup back to Ucolo Road, pulled into the brush, and waited for Boris to arrive in his vehicle. He looked at his watch. He had over an hour to kill. No problem. He was good at sitting and waiting.

Boris arrived right on schedule and motioned for Dimitri to follow him. They drove south on Ucolo Road to its intersection with U.S. 491, turned right, and drove toward the Abajo Mountains. They turned left at Monticello and continued south on U.S. 191 through the towns of Blanding and Bluff. Just south of Bluff, they crossed the bridge over the San Juan River and entered the Navajo reservation. They drove through the sandy scrub brush country for several miles, finally turning left onto a dirt road that climbed to the top of Casa Del Eco Mesa. Dimitri wondered where Boris was leading him. After several more turns onto roads of successively diminishing quality, Boris stopped. He got out of his pickup and hobbled back to Dimitri. Dimitri rolled down the window.

"Pull the truck off the road, shut off the engine, and leave the key in the ignition. Remove the license plates. Then gather up any identification papers in the vehicle. Look everywhere. In the glove compartment, under the seat, behind the seat, above the sun visors, in the ash tray. Wrap everything in the tarp and put it in my pickup." Boris handed him a screwdriver.

Dimitri unscrewed the license plates and removed all the papers from the pickup. Then Boris handed him a rag and told him to wipe away all surfaces where he might have left fingerprints. Dimitri did so.

On the drive back to the ranch, Boris stopped in Bluff at the Desert Rose Motel and pulled up next to the dumpster. "Dimitri, throw the tarp and everything from the truck into the dumpster."

That done, they headed back to the ranch. Dimitri looked at Boris. "When Navajos find pickup, won't they tell authorities?"

"Probably not. Most likely, they'll consider it a gift from the spirits. Pretty soon, it'll be hauling firewood to their hogans in preparation for winter."

Dimitri frowned. Boris always seemed so damned sure of himself. Dimitri decided to change the subject. He pointed to the two laptop computers on the seat between them. "What are those?"

"They're computers," said Boris. "I'm in charge of the organization's finances. Those computers keep records of all our investments. I'm never without them."

Dimitri nodded. "Is Dimitri's work finished?"

"Yes. Well, maybe not entirely. There's a cop named Rivera who's been sniffing around. He might be on our trail. I'll call the boss later and see what he wants to do next."

An hour later they were back at the ranch. "Your work here is done, Dimitri. You can go now," said Boris. "I'll call the boss and fill him in."

Dimitri walked to his four-wheel-drive green Range Rover, hoisted himself into the cab, and drove out of the ranch. He headed for Monticello to get a room for the night.

He was irritated. He worked directly for the boss and he didn't need Boris to do his reporting for him.

When he pulled into the parking lot of the Canyonlands Motor Inn, he dialed the boss's number on his cell phone. It was late but the boss wouldn't mind.

"Boss, it's Dimitri. Job is done. I'm in Monticello."

"Good, Dimitri. We've taken care of the Newark end of the job too." He laughed a sinister laugh. "Who do these amateurs think they're dealing with?" He laughed again, louder this time. "Okay Dimitri, I want you to stay in Monticello. Check into a motel and wait until you hear from me. I may have another job for you to do up there."

"Yes, boss. I wait to hear from you."

Dimitri checked into the motel, paying cash and using an alias. He liked staying in motels. The longer, the better.

He located his room, unlocked the door, and entered. Before doing anything else, he turned on the television and began flipping through the channels. He found an old black and white movie on the TCM channel and lay down on the bed. He hoped the boss would leave him here for a few days. He loved watching television. He could do it all day long. Often did. Soap operas were his favorite, especially the Hispanic soap operas. He couldn't understand anything they were saying but he liked looking at the women.

He wondered why the boss wanted him to stay in Monticello. A pleasant thought occurred to him. Maybe his next job would be the cop named Rivera.

30

RIVERA THOUGHT ABOUT IT all night and again this morning, but it still made no sense. He couldn't understand why the FBI didn't want him to pick up Boris Petrov yesterday evening. Now it was Saturday morning and Sheriff Bradshaw was explaining it to him again. The Feds were scheduled to arrive for a meeting at eight o'clock, so Rivera and his boss only had a few more minutes to discuss the matter.

"They want to pick him up themselves," Bradshaw was saying. "They're sending agents down from Salt Lake City to accomplish the arrest. Boris Petrov is very important to them. He escaped their net once and they're not about to let it happen again."

Bradshaw had explained this to Rivera last night after his phone conversation with Agent Bowers in Salt Lake City. But Rivera still didn't get it. "So why the big meeting?"

"I'm guessing they'll want to use us as backup. Our job will be to set up road blocks around the county before they move in on Petrov. Just in case he eludes them again and tries to escape. They'll probably use state cops to set up check points all over the Four Corners region. They won't be taking any chances this time. I'm sure they'll want us to cover the back roads, especially the roads through the LaSal Mountains into Colorado."

Rivera considered that for a moment. Shook his head. Then decided to just accept it. "What makes Petrov so important?"

"There were probably lots of red faces when he slipped away in 1996. The FBI doesn't like to be embarrassed. I guess they feel more confident making the arrest themselves, even though they failed the first time. Carl Bowers told me last night that Petrov, being a financial guy for the Russian Mafia, has plenty of knowledge about the mob's activities all over the country. He launders their money and then invests it in legitimate enterprises. Carl said if they'd caught him in Brooklyn back in 1996, they would have offered him a deal in exchange for information. So if they catch him this time, they'll probably make the same offer. If he agrees to testify against the mob, he'll likely receive a new life complete with a new identity. *Another* new identity."

"Where does this leave us? Am I still in charge of the case or is the FBI taking over?"

"I think we have two separate cases. Petrov couldn't be Flanagan's killer because of his handicap. So there's still an unidentified killer on the loose out there. The

FBI is looking for Petrov and we're looking for the shooter. Since it's likely Petrov hired the shooter, the two cases are intertwined. I think we'd better just wait and hear what the FBI has to say."

"I still think they should've let us arrest Petrov last night. Why take a chance on letting him slip away?"

"You're probably right. However, the FBI has an insatiable appetite for good publicity. An important arrest with newspaper and TV coverage goes a long way in that direction. It's especially valuable in Washington around budget time. If we made the arrest without them, they'd lose an opportunity to look good in the eyes of Congress."

Rivera wanted to comment on that but decided there was no point. He'd just sound like he was complaining. "When I visited Meriwether Williams in his office, he was working with two laptop computers. If he was managing the mob's money, those computers might contain information about their financial operations. I think we should tell the FBI to be on the lookout for them."

"Good idea, Manny." Bradshaw pushed himself out of his chair and walked over to the window. Peered outside. "It looks like our friends are arriving now. Best not to say too much during the meeting. Let them tell us what they want us to know. Answer their questions. Be real helpful. The FBI frowns on local cops who aren't cooperative. If they want to, they can cause us a lot of trouble. So just figure for the time being we work for them." Bradshaw looked at Rivera and smiled. "And don't forget, they make twice as much money as you do."

31

BORIS PETROV DROVE HIS tan Ford Explorer north on U.S. 191 toward Moab after spending the night at the ranch. He was reflecting on what he'd done yesterday and not feeling very good about it. He'd never gotten to know February Flanagan or William Reynolds as individuals. So having them killed seemed like an impersonal act. Kind of like playing a board game. But during the brief period he'd spent talking to Bart Winslow, he found himself liking him and, in a way, admiring him. He seemed like a good kid. Under different circumstances, he would have enjoyed getting to know him better. Maybe even mentoring him. Or partnering with him. His computer skills would have come in handy. Boris wondered if he would ever be able to forget the sound of Dimitri's handgun firing that single shot, followed by the thump of Bart's body hitting the ground. The suddenness with which a life could be terminated made him feel a certain vulnerability.

Despite his feelings of guilt, Boris was relieved the ordeal was over. Maybe now his life could return to normal.

When he'd called Claire last night, she promised him a ham-and-eggs breakfast as soon as he got home. He'd grown very close to her since their wedding six years ago He didn't like spending even a single night away from her. When he first married her, he did it as part of his cover. He needed to look the part of a respectable businessman. And it didn't hurt that she was well connected, having been born into wealth and politics. But during the past few years, an unexpected closeness had developed. She wasn't a beautiful woman but she was smart, attentive, good natured, and fun to be around. He thought about her during his workday and often called her on the phone just to chat. He looked forward to going home and spending the evening with her. He often wondered what his life would have been like if he hadn't been born the son of a Russian Mafia man, if instead he'd been born into a normal family, become a CPA, and met Claire early in life. He enjoyed the financial aspects of his job and found them interesting and challenging. But he didn't like working with criminals. Or being one.

After filling his gas tank at the Shell station south of town, he drove into Moab and turned right on Center Street. One block later his heart sunk. Parked in front of the Sheriff's Department building were four black

Ford Crown Victoria automobiles. A dead giveaway the FBI had arrived. His mind started racing. That cop Rivera must have somehow gotten on to him. Now he had to run. And fast. But where? They would be organizing roadblocks all over Utah to look for his vehicle. If he went north to I-70, they'd have no trouble finding him on the interstate whether he headed east or west. If he went south back through Monticello, he could head for southwest Colorado, northwest New Mexico, or northeast Arizona. But he'd be an easy pickup there too because he'd be on U.S. highways the whole way. What about the Navajo reservation? It was huge and remote with thousands of backcountry roads, but he'd be exposed during the two hours it would take to get there. He considered heading east on the back roads through the LaSal Mountains, but there were only a few exit roads into Colorado and they'd be too easy to cover. He could head west across back roads, but the Colorado River gorge would eventually block his escape. The river! That's it! His heart was pounding. He needed to get his kayak but he didn't dare go home. They would be watching his house. Then he remembered. He'd brought his kayak to Johnson's Rafting Company after the last race to get a few dings repaired. He drove north out of town and pulled into Johnson's parking lot. His red and white kayak was in the rack out front and it looked like the repairs had been completed. He loaded it on top of his vehicle and tied it down with bungee cords. Just then, Slim Johnson appeared in the doorway.

"She's all set to go, Meriwether. Your gear is packed inside her."

"Thanks, Slim. Send me a bill, okay?"

"Sure, no problem."

Boris and Slim had been good friends ever since Boris started kayaking. He began paddling on the Colorado River solely to get some cardiovascular exercise. Because of his leg, he couldn't run or even walk very far. So kayaking was an ideal solution. Slim sold him a kayak and taught him how to handle it. Turned out he had an aptitude for it. One day Slim suggested Boris try competitive racing. As the years passed, Boris developed a love for the sport as well as increased endurance and upper body strength. Soon he was a champion kayaker. Boris felt a sadness as he drove out of the parking lot knowing he'd never see Slim again.

He crossed the bridge that spanned the Colorado River and headed north, checking the rearview mirror as he drove. After a short distance, he turned left on the Potash Road and followed it alongside the west bank of the river. Initially his thinking was to launch in the Colorado and head downriver into the canyons. Then he thought better of it. The Colorado was a popular waterway for rafting and kayaking because it passed right through town and was easily accessible via paved roads. Larger tour boats often carried the less adventuresome visitors up and down the river to see parts of the canyon country inaccessible by road. There was always a lot of boat traffic on the Colorado. Too many curious eyes.

The Green River was far less popular for boating. It was remote and accessible only by traversing miles of dirt roads across a mesa and then descending tricky switchbacks to the river level. Petrov knew a way to get to the Green River on roads the Feds were unlikely to cover. None of the roads he had in mind would seem to the FBI like escape routes from Moab.

The Green eventually fed into the Colorado, but the confluence was so far downriver that when he finally arrived at the Colorado, it was unlikely he'd see other boaters. There was much less traffic that far downriver from Moab.

He sped down the pavement of the Potash Road until he reached the Long Canyon cutoff. He turned right onto a dirt road and carefully followed its switchbacks up through Pucker Pass. His emotions toggled between fear and regret. Fear that he'd get caught and spend the rest of his years in prison surrounded by a bunch of uneducated animals like Dimitri, and regret that he'd just lost the life he loved. And the woman he loved.

He navigated under a huge slab of Wingate sandstone which had fallen from the mesa top eons ago. It was leaning against the canyon wall, creating a triangular tunnel through which the road passed. The road was narrow with a sharp drop-off to his right. He drove slowly, carefully. He hoped he wouldn't meet another vehicle coming downhill. The uphill driver had the right-of-way but not everyone knew the rule. He couldn't afford any delays. After another long series of switchbacks, he finally made it to the top of the mesa. He sped west on a graded dirt road. Hopefully, he thought, the Feds wouldn't be looking for him up here.

32

SHERIFF LEROY BRADSHAW SURVEYED the conference room. At the head of the table was Phil Lisowski who had been sent from Washington to handle the arrest of Boris Petrov. Bradshaw had spoken with him briefly in his office prior to the meeting. Born in Chicago, Lisowski had spent most of his career in the Chicago and New York offices of the FBI. His specialty was racketeering and mob crime. He was a part of the team that had raided the Brooklyn Marine Terminal in 1996. After a series of promotions, he was now a Special Agent who reported directly to the Deputy Director of the FBI. Bradshaw, who'd met his share of FBI agents over the years, sized him up as smart and political. Bradshaw guessed his age to be early fifties. He had a medium build and wore a charcoal suit with a conservative blue and silver striped tie. His hair was dark brown except around the temples, the result of carefully applied hair coloring as best Bradshaw could tell. Lisowski was a city boy out of his element.

Sitting around the table were Sheriff Anthony Zilic of San Juan County, the Moab Chief of Police Andy Simms, BLM Investigative Agent Adam Dunne, National Park Service Ranger Mario Garza, and a state cop Rivera had never seen before. Five well-groomed clean-shaven FBI agents in dark suits rounded out those sitting at the table. Manny Rivera and three other Grand County deputy sheriffs sat in chairs against the wall due to the limited size of the conference room table.

"Thank you for coming this morning," Lisowski began. He spoke with a Chicago accent. "Last night, Sheriff Bradshaw called FBI Agent Carl Bowers in Salt Lake City and informed him that Boris Petrov was living here in Moab. He'd been a resident for about six years and had assumed the alias Richard Meriwether Williams. Washington assigned the case to me. I'm here with agents from the Salt Lake City and Farmington offices." He gestured toward the men in dark suits. They sat motionless with neutral expressions. "Let me start by saying how important Boris Petrov is to us. He is the financial brains behind a large segment of Russian Mafia operations in the United States. His specialty is international money laundering. His associates are wanted for murder, extortion, dealing in arms, theft, blackmail, hijacking, and especially drug running and distribution. They have strong ties with two Mexican drug gangs, the Zetas and the Sinaloa Cartel. They are dangerous people and, make no mistake about it, they will kill at the drop of a hat. If we can apprehend Petrov and convince him it's in his best interest to work with us, we'll have taken a giant step in busting a major crime ring in the United States." He paused for effect. "The most important thing I want to communicate this morning is this: We want him alive. Under no circumstances is he to be killed. We just need to find him and apprehend him."

Bradshaw glanced at his deputies while Lisowski spoke. All but Rivera wore matter-of-fact expressions. They were paying attention but in a detached way. Rivera looked concerned. Probably because he realized that men in dark suits driving Black Ford Crown Vics would be noticed in a small town like Moab, particularly by an experienced criminal. And Rivera didn't want Petrov to escape, now that he'd identified him. Bradshaw was proud of Rivera and the job he'd done. When Bradshaw hired him four years ago, he wasn't sure about his investigative capabilities. Rivera was smart and competent as a law enforcement officer, but he'd had little experience in detective work. But over the past few years he'd proven himself. Now he was as good as any deputy in the county. Probably one of the best. Bradshaw had underestimated him, which was easy to do because of his low-key manner and calm demeanor.

Lisowski continued. "As of a few minutes ago, we have his house and office under surveillance. As yet there's been no sign of him coming or going. After this meeting is concluded and our roadblocks are in place, we'll move in on both locations. He also owns a ranch in San Juan County. We have agents ready to move in down there as well.

"Sheriff Bradshaw has informed me that Petrov may have two laptop computers in his possession. It's likely they contain information about mob operations and finances. We want the computers, so be on the lookout for same. Sheriff Bradshaw also informed me that Petrov became handicapped sometime since our encounter with him in Brooklyn. He now moves about on a cane so he's not likely to escape on foot." Lisowski looked at his notepad. "Petrov's vehicle is a 2009 tan Ford Explorer SUV." He read off the license plate number which was duly recorded by each man present. Then he discussed the roadblock assignments: State cops on state highways, county cops on backcountry roads, FBI agents in town with Moab City cops assisting, BLM and National Park personnel in their respective areas of responsibility, FBI agents from Colorado, New Mexico, and Arizona at the state lines. A package of maps was handed to each man in the room showing the desired roadblock locations. Further instructions regarding communications frequencies and protocols were provided. The plan was set to go into effect at 0930 Hours. In a coordinated move, Petrov's home, office, and ranch would be raided and searched. If he was not found at any of these locations, all law enforcement personnel would be notified immediately and a manhunt would ensue.

Bradshaw had heard all this before. Dozens of times on previous cases where the FBI was involved. This type of approach probably worked well in big cities, but it didn't make much sense in southeast Utah. Rivera was right. Petrov should have been picked up yesterday.

Bradshaw's thoughts turned to his wife. He wanted to be spending time with her instead of sitting in pointless meetings like this one. But she'd insisted he "continue life normally." "Someday soon I'll be gone," she'd told him while holding his hand tightly, "and you'll be sad, but Moab will still need a good man as sheriff." But how the hell would he be able to *continue life normally?* Every night coming home to an empty house. No one to talk to. No one to be with. No one to love. Maybe after Jill was gone, he would just leave Moab and try to start over somewhere else. Too many memories here.

"Lastly, I want to repeat: We need Petrov alive," said Lisowski. "Now, are there any questions?"

Bradshaw glanced at Rivera. His normally relaxed face looked anxious. He shifted in his chair and looked like he wanted to say something. But he remained silent.

33

BORIS PETROV CONTINUED ACROSS the mesa top in his SUV. He was shaking and felt as though he was going to cry, something he hadn't done since he was a little boy. He pounded the steering wheel and wondered how he could have so totally screwed up his life. He didn't kill those three men, but he was responsible for their deaths. Same as if he'd pulled the trigger himself. What had happened to him? When had he become a monster? He came over a rise and saw the dirt road he was driving on connected to a two-lane paved road which would lead to Dead Horse Point State Park if he turned left. He turned right. He continued on the pavement for about three miles and turned left on Mineral Bottom Road, a dirt road that would take him across twelve miles of remote undulating backcountry to the Green River.

He needed a plan. The FBI would be scouring the county looking for him on the roads. He doubted they would think to check the rivers. Unfortunately, that deputy named Rivera knew he was a champion kayaker. But Rivera, if he thought of a kayak escape at all, would probably think in terms of the Colorado River since it ran right through Moab. Petrov's mind was buzzing with questions. How far would he paddle? Where would he leave the river? What would he do then? There were miles and miles of escape routes on both sides of the river. Scores of side canyons, each of which was fed by a multitude of tributary canyons. He might have to survive on his own for a long time. He reminded himself to load into the kayak the water jugs and snack bars he routinely kept in his SUV.

He looked in his rearview mirror and saw he was leaving a plume of dust in his wake. He eased off the gas pedal and reduced his speed. He didn't want to attract any undue attention. His thoughts returned to the river. Should he paddle downriver a few miles, hide the kayak, and hike into a side canyon? Or should he continue down the river, past its confluence with the Colorado, and keep going? But then what? If he continued on, he would have to make it through Cataract Canyon, something he'd never attempted before.

The rapids of Cataract Canyon were Level IV, which meant they were extremely turbulent, even violent in places. They could be heard a half-mile upriver. The river would be moving fast with incredible force, flowing downhill at a slope noticeable to the naked eye. There would be long, repeating, powerful rapids passing between dangerous rocks. All along the way there would be whirlpools and boiling eddies. Standing waves fifteen feet high and holes in the water just as deep required expert boatmanship. One miscalculation and he could be smashed against the rocks.

Petrov's kayaking experience never included Level IV rapids. The Colorado River races seldom passed through rapids exceeding Level I. He had strength and stamina for distance racing but had little experience in scouting and navigating serious rapids. He'd learned how to right a capsized kayak, using body motion and paddle, but he'd never tried it in intensely turbulent water. Despite all the dangers, running Cataract Canyon in a kayak was something he'd always wanted to try.

On the other hand, he could hide the kayak and hike up a side canyon. It would be difficult with his damaged leg, but maybe it was possible. Just go slowly and step carefully. There he'd be taking a different kind of risk. He could get lost, run out of water, die of thirst. He had two one-gallon plastic milk containers filled with water in his vehicle. That would be enough for two or three days. Maybe he could stretch it to four. If he hiked out on the east side of the river, he'd be back in Grand County. Not a good idea. If he hiked west, he'd be outside Grand County but smack in the middle of the Maze, an aptly named riot of interconnected canyons. He remembered hearing stories of people who had hiked into the Maze and were never seen again.

But he had to be realistic. He was really in no condition to hike any significant distance. His leg wouldn't permit it. Maybe he could make it a quarter-mile or so, find a cave or an overhang, and camp out until the heat was off. But how would he know when the heat was off? And what would he do then?

It seemed like both options were bad. There was a third possibility, of course. He could turn himself in to the FBI and agree to testify in exchange for leniency. If he did, there was a risk the mob would eventually find him and kill him. Dimitri would volunteer to do the job pro bono.

All things considered, he judged that running the rapids through Cataract Canyon was his best shot. If he could make it downriver to Lake Powell, he could leave the river at the Hite Crossing Bridge and climb the trail up to the road. There was a primitive landing strip on the west side of the bridge. If the boss was willing to help him one more time, he might arrange to have a private plane or a vehicle waiting for him there. It would take two days of paddling to reach the bridge but if he paced himself and rested at regular intervals, he should be able to do it. He picked up his cell phone and looked at it. There were two bars showing. He stopped the vehicle, shut off the engine, and got out. He dialed the boss's number.

The conversation went better than expected. The boss understood the situation, agreed with Boris's decision to leave Moab immediately, and promised to have a vehicle waiting for him at the Hite Crossing Bridge in two days. Boris would be driven to Tucson and hidden in an apartment there until they figured out what to do next. The boss asked about the computers and seemed relieved that Boris still had them in his possession.

Boris got back into his SUV and drove the remaining five miles to the edge of the bluff overlooking the Green River. He got out of his vehicle and took one last look around the mesa. It was probably a scene he would never lay eyes on again. A profound emptiness engulfed him as he climbed back into his vehicle and started the engine. He was leaving a life he loved and the suddenness of the decision made the pain even more unbearable. His thoughts were about Claire as he slowly descended the switchbacks to the river.

When he reached the bottom, he drove his vehicle upriver on a primitive road until he found a break in the thick tamarisk that lined the banks. He nosed his SUV into the dense brush and drove forward to the bank of the river. He unhooked the bungee cords and removed the kayak and paddle from the roof rack. Then he placed the two laptop computers into a waterproof rubber pack and sealed it. He removed the water, food, and a hat from the vehicle and packed them and the computers into the kayak. He slipped on the life jacket stowed in the kayak and carefully lowered himself into the craft, using his cane for support.

He pushed off and began paddling downriver, sadly hoping for the best.

34

DEPUTY SHERIFF EMMETT MITCHELL was cruising east on U.S. 491, listening to a new Billie Holiday CD he'd just received as a gift from his wife. He loved the old jazz classics. He was on his way to Eastland to check on a vandalism report. A pinto bean farmer had claimed his John Deere 7030 tractor had been spray painted with graffiti. Mitchell knew the trip was pointless. The kid who tagged the tractor would be long gone and unless he autographed his masterpiece, there would be no way to identify the culprit. Keeping the citizens of San Juan County happy was part of the job. That included listening to pinto bean farmers demanding justice and better police protection. But what the heck, it was a nice day for a drive and Billie was singing *Don't Explain* like no one else could.

His cell phone buzzed. He turned down the volume on the CD player. It was the San Juan County Sheriff's Office dispatcher. Since she had called on Mitchell's cell phone instead of his police-band radio, the subject matter would be sensitive.

"Emmett, we just received a call from a couple of hikers in Summit Canyon. They found a body at the base of a bluff a couple of miles east of Ucolo Road. Victim was apparently shot in the head and dumped into the canyon. Sheriff Zilic wants you to handle it. The hikers are waiting at the scene." She gave him the GPS coordinates for the cutoff to the canyon.

"I'm on my way."

Mitchell switched on his light bar, drove to Ucolo Road, and headed north. He located the cutoff road, turned right, and bounced down the dirt road until he reached Summit Canyon. He pulled his vehicle to a stop and walked to the edge of the bluff. At the bottom of the canyon, he saw the body. Some distance away, he saw two hikers sitting on the ground. They stood up and waved when they spotted him.

Mitchell walked along the edge of the bluff until he found a primitive cattle trail that led to the bottom. He carefully descended the trail. The small stones that littered the surface of the steep slope had a tendency to slide under the weight of his footsteps. He grasped the bushes alongside the trail to steady himself during the descent.

One of the hikers was an older man, paunchy, probably in his sixties. The other was in his twenties with a boyish freckled face. Both were wearing Boy Scout uniforms. Mitchell introduced himself and asked who they were.

"I'm the Scout Master of Boy Scout Troop #16 in Farmington and this is one of my Assistant Scout Masters," said the older man. He stated their names which Mitchell recorded in his notepad. "We took the boys on a hike up Summit Canyon from the Dolores River yesterday. They're camped out about a half-mile east of here. Two of my other assistants are with them now. Last night around eight o'clock we heard a loud crack up-canyon from our camp. We were curious about the noise. It was too dark to explore then but this morning after breakfast, Bill and I decided to take a look. We were especially interested when we noticed a few buzzards circling up this way. Anyway, we found that body." He pointed. "We checked for a pulse. Didn't find one. Looks like he was shot in the head and dumped off the rim of the canyon. The crack we heard must have been the cottonwood limb the body broke on the way down. Bill here climbed up to the rim so he could get a cell phone signal and call it in. He went up on the same trail you used to get down here."

Mitchell walked over and inspected the dead man. He was lying face-up with his arms and legs outspread. A line of dried blood ran across the forehead, leading from what appeared to be a bullet hole in the right temple. The corpse had a surprised look on its face.

He reached into the rear pants pocket and slid out a billfold. He read the name on the driver's license: Bart Winslow from Moab. He recognized the name. Manny

Rivera had mentioned it during one of their morning breakfasts at the Rim Rock Diner. He was a person of interest in Rivera's investigation.

After encircling the area around the corpse with yellow crime scene tape, Mitchell climbed back to the top of the bluff. He taped off the area on the rim directly above the corpse to protect any footprints which may have been left by the killer at the edge of the bluff. Then he called his office, requesting crime scene support and the Medical Examiner. Finally, he dialed Rivera at his office.

"Hi, Emmett. I just got out of a meeting with some FBI visitors. I can't talk now. I'll fill you in on the details later but right now I've got to leave. I'm on my way into the LaSals for roadblock duty."

"Hold on, Manny. This isn't a social call. I've got something important to tell you. We just found a corpse in Summit Canyon down here. Murdered and then dumped into the canyon. A single shot to the temple. Probably happened around nightfall yesterday. The victim's name is Bart Winslow. From Moab."

35

RIVERA HASTILY ENTERED BRADSHAW'S office and closed the door. The sheriff looked up from the file he was reading. "Aren't you supposed to be headed toward the LaSals?"

"Yes, but there's been a new development. Emmett Mitchell just called. Bart Winslow's body was found in Summit Canyon a little while ago. He was shot in the head."

Bradshaw sat back in his chair and folded his arms. He was silent for a moment, then shook his head. "What's happened to this little town of ours?" He stood up and walked to the window. Stared outside. "You'd better tell the family. I'll call Sheriff Zilic and suggest you and Emmett form a joint task force to concentrate on finding Bart's killer. I'm sure Zilic will agree. I'll assign Dave Tibbetts to the backcountry roadblock detail to take your place."

Rivera paused, considered his unwelcome assignment. "Any advice on how to tell the Winslows? What do I say?"

Bradshaw was still looking out the window. "There's no easy way to do it, Manny. Just tell them their son is dead. Tell them how it happened."

Rivera climbed into his vehicle and reluctantly drove toward the Winslow residence, hoping each traffic light along the way would be red. There was no way to soften the crushing blow he would be delivering to a family who'd already lost a son in Iraq. Rivera had never before been assigned to communicate the death of a child to its family. He felt a numbness of body and spirit.

He rang the doorbell. He removed his hat, held it with both hands, and waited.

Mrs. Winslow answered the door. She was a thin grey-haired woman with dark eyes. "Good morning, Deputy." There was fear in her voice as if she was expecting bad news. "Bart never came home last night."

Rivera hesitated. He hadn't anticipated that Mrs. Winslow would answer the door. He was expecting to see her husband. Should he tell her or ask for Mr. Winslow? "Um...Is Henry...uh... at home?" he stammered. "I need to talk to him...to you both...together." He knew he must have a very pained look on his face.

"He's back in his office." Her hand trembled as she pulled the door all the way open, eyes locked onto Rivera's. She stepped aside and motioned for him to pass, her eyes becoming moist.

Rivera walked down the hallway, Mrs. Winslow following closely behind him. He tapped on the office doorjamb. Henry Winslow was listening to music and typing on his computer keyboard. He looked up.

Rivera stepped into the office followed by Mrs. Winslow, tears now flowing down her cheeks. "I'm afraid I have some terrible news."

After Rivera provided them with the details of their son's death, he awkwardly asked for the key to Bart's cabin, explaining he needed access as part of the investigation into Bart's death. A stunned Henry Winslow, never taking his eyes off his wife, silently reached into his pocket and handed Rivera a key ring. Rivera took it and left as the Winslows fell into each other's arms.

He felt a pain in the pit of his stomach as he walked back to Bart's cabin. If only he'd found Bart yesterday, he might still be alive today. Why hadn't he put more effort into the search around town? He unlocked the door, entered, and sat down in the chair in front of Bart's desk. Bart's radio was still on, tuned to KZMU. The DJ was announcing that the next song would be Guy Clark's *The Guitar*. It was an eerie feeling, being in the home of a man who had just died. It was almost as though Rivera could still sense Bart's presence in the cabin. He shook off the feeling and took a moment to think about his new assignment. It seemed obvious that Petrov was responsible for Bart's death. Petrov had February Flanagan killed in order to keep his identity secret. Then he had William Reynolds killed for the same reason. It was now beyond any doubt that Bart had created and sold the false identities. He must have sold one to Petrov, and Petrov, in a further attempt to protect his identity, had Bart killed as well. Rivera didn't understand the timing of Bart's murder. Why now? Why not three years ago when Flanagan was killed? The answer must have been that Petrov had only recently become aware of Bart's role in the false identity business.

Rivera closed the laptop computer on Bart's desk and unplugged it from the wall. Certainly there was a good chance that critical information establishing Bart's role in creating the identities would be stored in the computer. He would take it back to the office so Sheriff Bradshaw could present it to Agent Lisowski. The FBI had its faults, but no one was better equipped to analyze the contents of Bart's computer and understand the implications of the information it contained.

Rivera picked up the phone on Bart's desk and dialed Mitchell's cell-phone number. He answered on the first ring.

"Emmett, it's Manny. Did Sheriff Zilic talk to you?"

"Yeah. He wants us to collaborate on the Bart Winslow case."

"Right, but I'm certain Boris Petrov, alias Meriwether Williams of Moab, is the guilty party. Most likely he called in a hit man from the mob to kill Bart Winslow. Petrov is the one we want but the FBI is calling the shots. The Agent-in-Charge is used to conducting big city investigations. He thinks he knows what he's doing out here but I'm not so sure. Things are a lot different in the backcountry."

"So what's our next step?" asked Mitchell.

"I'm at the Winslow residence. I notified the family and now I'm in Bart's cabin picking up his computer. I think it will verify that Bart originated Petrov's alias. And the FBI will probably be interested in all the other aliases Bart created. When I leave here I'm heading back to the office."

"I'm still at the crime scene. We're casting footprints at the top of the cliff. The Medical Examiner is down in the canyon with the body. It looks like Bart was shot in the head with a small-caliber slug. I'm betting it's going to be a match for the slugs in the two killings you've been investigating."

"I wouldn't be surprised. Okay, Emmett, I'll check back with you later."

Rivera hung up the phone and then dialed a second number. There was no escaping the fact that his date with Vivian Ramos tonight would have to be postponed. He drummed his fingers on the desk as the phone rang four times. There was a click and the answering machine came on. It was a generic telephone company message in a male voice. He reluctantly left a message saying he would be on duty twenty-four seven until the case was wrapped up. He would call her as soon as that happened. He told her how much he regretted not being able to see her tonight and how disappointed he was.

That done, he picked up Bart's computer and left the Winslow residence.

When he arrived back at the office, he learned from Millie Ives that Petrov had not been found at his home, office, or ranch. Rivera wasn't at all surprised.

36

RIVERA WAS BACK at his desk, trying to overcome the irritation caused by Petrov's escape. He worked hard to keep his mind focused on the problem instead of Lisowski's ham-handed attempt at an arrest. Roadblocks had been set up everywhere and all airports were being watched, even the private airstrips. State cops in New Mexico, Arizona, and Colorado were now part of the manhunt as were the tribal police of the Ute, Uintah, Navajo, Hopi, and Apache nations. Petrov was nowhere to be found and neither was his vehicle.

Rivera wondered how it was possible Petrov hadn't been spotted yet. His wife Claire had said he'd called early this morning on his way back to town from the ranch. He'd told her he was filling up his gas tank at the Shell station and this had been verified by the credit card company. That was at seven-fifty this morning, so he couldn't have gotten very far in the big empty landscape of southeast Utah. Petrov had escaped the FBI's clutches once before so he was probably fairly skilled at evading his pursuers. He probably spotted the black

267

Crown Vics and left town immediately. And it must have happened while that pompous Lisowski was lecturing the local cops on his grand plan for capturing Petrov.

Rivera put himself in Petrov's place. Where would he go if he had to leave town undetected on extremely short notice? He opened his desk drawer and removed a set of maps covering southeast Utah. He unfolded a Grand County map and scanned the paved roads out of Moab. They'd all been covered by the Utah State Police. And deputies were covering the backcountry roads exiting Grand County. So it seemed unlikely he would try to escape simply by driving out of the county. Was it possible he was still in Grand County? He could have driven to some remote place and just hidden out. Possibly in the LaSal Mountains. Or the area around Yellow Cat Flat. There were plenty of abandoned mining roads back in there. Or the Kokopelli Trail area around Rose Garden Hill. If Petrov had enough food and water, he could last for weeks in some remote arroyo and never be seen by a soul.

Rivera's eyes fell on the Colorado River. Petrov was a champion kayaker. Was it conceivable he would try to escape by river? The Colorado flowed from the Rocky Mountains into Utah, through Moab, and on to Lake Powell and the Glen Canyon Dam. If he did attempt a river escape, he'd have to stay on the river until he arrived at a place where he could hike a short distance to a road and be picked up by an associate.

The first road crossing downriver from Moab was the Hite Crossing Bridge, over a hundred river miles away. Rivera wondered how fast Petrov could propel his kayak. He had no idea. It was also possible Petrov could paddle downriver a few miles, then hide the kayak and hike up a side canyon. Because of his leg, he wouldn't be able to hike very far. Probably less than a mile. He could possibly just hide and wait and hope the passage of time would cause the cops to give up on the hunt. If he had sufficient provisions, that seemed like a good plan. Would he have stopped at a grocery store and bought provisions after seeing the Crown Vics in town? Not likely. He would have been in too much of a hurry to get out of town.

Rivera continued studying the map. The Green River was also a possibility. It flowed south and joined the Colorado in the Needles District of Canyonlands National Park, about eighty miles downriver. Both rivers passed through deep red rock canyons with plenty of places where Petrov could hide out.

Rivera decided that since the roads and airports were all covered by other law enforcement personnel, he'd check the river theory himself. But how? And which river? There wouldn't be sufficient time to check them both. He had to choose one or the other. The Colorado was close and had easy access from Moab. The Green was remote and much more difficult to access. He studied the access points to the Green River.

The closest one to Moab was at the end of Mineral Bottom Road.

He called Jimmy Jensen, the old prospector from the Rim Rock Diner.

"Jimmy, this is Manny Rivera calling."

"Well, hello, Manny," his voice boomed through the telephone. "Am I under arrest?" He let out a loud Santa-like laugh.

"Jimmy, is Freddie still out there staking a claim near Mineral Bottom Road?" Rivera pulled the phone a few inches from his ear and awaited the response.

"Yes indeedy. He's out there every day with his dog. He's measuring distances, driving stakes, and adding up his imaginary profits." Another loud laugh.

"Does he carry a cell phone?"

"Oh, sure. We prospectors might be old, but we are well acquainted with the marvels of modern technology." He gave Rivera the number.

Rivera dialed it and waited. After three rings he got an answer.

"Hello."

"Freddie, this is Manny Rivera calling."

"Hi, Manny." He sounded tired.

"Freddie, I have a very important question to ask you. Did you see an SUV carrying a kayak drive by on Mineral Bottom Road this morning?"

"Yes, I did. About two hours ago one came by headed for the river. It had a kayak mounted on the roof."

"Do you remember what make of vehicle it was? And what color?"

"I wasn't close enough to the road to tell you the make, but it was definitely an SUV. The color looked like tan. Of course, some of that might have been road dust."

"What about the color of the kayak?"

"Yeah. That I can tell you. It was mostly red with a white band in the middle."

"Okay, thanks, Freddie. That's a big help."

37

BORIS WORKED at a steady pace, trying to control his anxiety, forcing himself not to paddle too fast. The kayak glided through the water, moving in a nearly perfect straight line, its speed augmented by the river's current. He estimated he was paddling at four miles per hour, his speed impeded by a mild headwind blowing up-canyon. The river was flowing at roughly three miles per hour, so his speed through the canyon was approximately seven miles per hour.

According to his map, he needed to cover 112 river miles before reaching the Hite Crossing Bridge. He formulated a plan as he paddled. He would alternate between paddling for half-an-hour and resting for half-an-hour. During the rest periods, the current would continue to propel him, with only minor course corrections required of him to keep the craft centered in the river. He would continue this pattern all during the daylight hours and sleep on a sand bar at night. If he could keep up the pace, and then survive the tumultuous rapids of Cataract Canyon, he would probably reach the bridge by five o'clock tomorrow afternoon.

He was glad he'd selected the Green River rather than the Colorado for his escape, even though the Colorado route would have been shorter. The Green was far less traveled by rafters and kayakers. There was a much lower chance he would encounter someone else on the river, someone who might recognize him.

Claire returned to his thoughts. When she learned what he'd done and what kind of man he really was, she would probably never forgive him. And who could blame her? He had totally ruined his life and probably hers too.

Regrets about the path he'd chosen in life resurfaced. If he hadn't followed his father's wishes and become part of "the brotherhood," he wouldn't have ended up in such a miserable state. He'd tasted the good life living with Claire in the Moab community but there was no way he could shake his past. He thought about how life was a long series of decisions, forks in the road, and how little thought he'd given to the choices he'd made at each fork. He wished he could go back in time and change some of those decisions. But he knew he couldn't. A flock of Canadian geese passed high above him, honking as they flew, following the canyon southward on their way to a warmer winter climate. He wished he could fly away with them.

"Damn," he shouted loudly. Echoes returned from the massive red rock canyon walls: "DAMN, Damn, damn." He'd been close to his father as a boy and loved him very much. But today he felt a palpable anger toward the man who'd raised him. How could he have allowed his son to choose a life of crime? What good was money if you had to be constantly looking over your shoulder? Hell, the things he enjoyed most in life cost him practically nothing. Reading or watching TV with Claire, kayaking with friends, managing investments. How foolish he'd been.

He paddled downriver with broad smooth strokes, his experience as a champion kayaker serving him well. He was on an emotional roller coaster, now blaming his father for the fix he was in, then feeling guilty for blaming the man who raised him, loved him, took him fishing, taught him how to throw a ball. Boris had made the decision to work for the mob as soon as he graduated from college. His father might have encouraged him, probably because he was proud of him and wanted his fellow mobsters to see how smart his son had become. But Boris had made the choice himself. And now he was responsible for whatever outcome the future would bring.

He wished he could talk to his father, but that was no longer an option. The man was gone. Boris found himself wondering who had killed him. Probably a hit man from a competing gang. Suddenly he stopped paddling. A troubling realization struck him. His father and the boss had shared power for decades. The boss had said they were like brothers, but the boss was ambitious and ruthless. Could he have had Boris's father killed? It was certainly possible. And if that were the case, Boris might be paddling into a dangerous situation.

He resumed paddling and reviewed his options. They boiled down to just two. Turn himself into the FBI and bargain for his freedom or trust the boss. For the next several miles, he re-evaluated those options. With the FBI, his knowledge of the gang's operations and finances were his only bargaining chip. In that case, the computers he was carrying were a liability. With the computers in hand, the Feds wouldn't need much information from him beyond what they would learn from the computers. His leverage would be gone. He'd do jail time and would no doubt be killed in prison. So for that option, the best course of action would be to dump the computers into the river and let them disappear into the silt at the bottom. Then he would be the sole source of information for the Feds.

He took that line of thought to the next level. If he related sufficient information to the feds and they set him free with a new identity, what then would he do? He'd have to find a job and earn a living. Probably in the world of investments. Somewhere where no one would recognize him. Maybe he could leave the country and go to a Caribbean island. Or even better, he could live in Paris.

That would require money, more money than he had. That's when the idea struck him. The bank access numbers for the mob accounts were in the computers and nowhere else. If he were able to make a deal with the FBI for his freedom, he could later move to Paris with his new identity and access the accounts. That would put several million dollars at his disposal. The mob would have no way of retrieving the money. He could simply move the cash to his own account. That meant the computers would have to be hidden somewhere in the canyon rather than tossed into the river. He'd have to retrieve them after the dust settled so he'd have all the account access numbers.

The second option was to trust the boss. Meet the vehicle at the Hite Crossing Bridge and hope he hadn't made the wrong decision. Hope is all it would be though, and he didn't like the idea of his life hanging on a thread of hope. He needed some insurance. The computers contained copious details about the mob's operations, details the boss wouldn't want to fall into the hands of the FBI. Hiding the computers in the canyon would work here too. He could simply tell the boss that he'd been worried about getting them through Cataract Canyon without damage and had hidden them in a safe place. He'd say he would go back and retrieve them after the heat was off. Then the boss would have to keep him alive. Boris would have time to size up the situation and decide if his life was in danger.

For both options the precaution was the same. Hide the computers. He would keep his eyes open for a suitable place in the canyon where they would be safe. He paddled downriver, scanning the cliff faces, realizing now he was all alone in the world.

* * *

Dimitri laughed heartily when the coyote ran off the cliff, remained suspended in mid-air with his legs still in a running motion, then looked down with a sheepish expression at his inevitable fate. The roadrunner had been victorious again. Dimitri took another bite from his candy bar and sat wide-eyed on the edge of his chair, waiting for the coyote to plunge to earth in a cloud of dust. The ringing of the motel room telephone instantly changed his mood. He hated to be interrupted in the middle of a cartoon.

"Hello."

"Dimitri, it's the boss. Time to go to work."

"Yes, boss. What Dimitri do next?"

"Tomorrow, go to the Hite Crossing Bridge. It's on Highway 95, right where the Colorado River runs into Lake Powell. Get there by two o'clock in the afternoon. Take the trail down to the river and wait for Boris to arrive in his kayak. When he arrives, take his two computers. Then kill him and drive back to Phoenix. I'll meet you there. If he doesn't have the computers with him, act real friendly and drive him to Phoenix so I can talk to him."

"Yes, boss."

"And call me either way."

"Yes, boss."

Dimitri hung up the phone and sat there thinking about tomorrow's assignment. He smiled at the thought of killing Boris. It would be payback for the way Boris had treated him over the years. Then he turned back to the TV and resumed watching cartoons.

38

RIVERA HADN'T YET SHARED his hunch of a river escape with the FBI or anyone else. There might be more than one red and white kayak in the county. He wanted to be sure he was on the right track before he called it in. If Petrov had launched his kayak on the Green River at Mineral Bottom, his vehicle would still be there. Rivera sped across Mineral Bottom Road dodging bumps and chug holes as best he could. He loved driving backcountry roads but not when he was in a hurry.

With three miles to go before he reached the river, Rivera spotted a pickup on the left side of the road. A small man and his dog were slowly walking through the brush out in a distant field. Rivera tooted his horn and waved as he went by. Freddie looked up and returned the wave.

When Rivera reached the rim of the bluff overlooking the river canyon, he stopped for a moment and surveyed the route. A steep road with a long series of switchbacks led down to the river level. Like all switchback roads, there was a sheer wall on one side and a dangerous precipice on the other. He shifted into four-wheel drive and began the descent. Ten minutes later he arrived at the bottom. The river bank was wide and lined with vegetation, primarily tamarisk. It reminded him of a lecture he'd attended one evening at the Moab Information Center. The subject was tamarisk. It was a thick bush which had been imported from central Asia and planted by the Army Corps of Engineers along western U.S. rivers to stabilizing their banks. With no natural predators, it thrived and spread rapidly. It grew so dense it became nearly impenetrable. A few years ago, it was declared a menace to the indigenous plant communities. Scientists then imported the tamarisk beetle from Central Asia to deal with the problem. Now the tamarisk had become much thinner.

That was the only reason Rivera was able to spot Petrov's vehicle. Petrov had pulled it into a thick tamarisk stand but because many of the branches had been defoliated by the voracious beetles, he'd seen the left rear fender. He checked the license number and made a cursory inspection of the vehicle. Loose bungee cords hung from the roof rack, confirming that Petrov had carried his kayak to this point. Rivera got back into his vehicle and drove back to the top of the mesa so he could call in the find. Neither his vehicle radio nor cell phone was capable of communicating from down in the canyon.

Back on top of the mesa, Rivera stepped out of his vehicle and dialed the sheriff's office from his cell phone. He heard nothing but static, now remembering he'd forgotten to buy a replacement battery for the phone. Irritated, he tossed the cell phone on the seat and made the call from his vehicle radio. He was breaking protocol by transmitting sensitive information over his radio instead of using his cell phone but he had no choice.

He informed Sheriff Bradshaw of the situation and estimated that Petrov had a head start of about two and a half hours. Bradshaw told him to return to the river bank and wait. He would contact the river rafting outfitters in town and find out if any of them had motorized rafts in the area. Bradshaw said that all commercial rafts were required by law to carry satellite phones in case emergency help was needed. They could all be contacted by their home offices. He would locate a nearby raft and send it to pick up Rivera so he could give chase. It wouldn't take long for a motorized raft to overtake a human-powered kayak, even with a head start of a few hours.

"The FBI said Petrov is likely unarmed but be careful anyway. They may be wrong about that," said Bradshaw.

Rivera hopped back into his vehicle, descended the switchbacks to the river level, and waited.

An hour later he heard an outboard motor. He looked upriver and saw a large rubber raft with a boatman and five passengers. As the raft drew closer, he recognized the boatman. It was Doug Mather from Moab. He waved as Doug brought the raft over to the river bank near an opening in the tamarisk.

"Hi, Manny. I've explained the situation to my passengers. Another raft is being sent down from the town of Green River to pick them up so they can continue their trip. They're going to the confluence and then back upriver to Moab on the Colorado." He turned to his passengers. "Okay, folks. Time to get off and have lunch."

Doug, a lean thirty-something with light brown hair and a blond mustache, removed the food, drinks, and a propane grill from the raft and found a volunteer among the passengers to serve as cook. All were understanding of the situation and even a little excited to see a real police chase up close. One of the men, a Viet Nam veteran, volunteered to come along and help. His offer was declined.

After he unloaded a small folding table for the food, Doug restarted the engine. He handed a life jacket to Rivera and instructed him to put it on. Then they took off. Doug brought the craft to the center of the river and slowly accelerated to a speed of twenty miles per hour. He looked at Rivera and smiled. "No kayaker in the world can maintain this speed."

"Sorry to interrupt the trip. But this is an emergency. We're chasing a felon by the name of Boris

Petrov. He's in a red and white kayak. You may know him by his alias: Meriwether Williams."

Doug looked surprised. "I do know him. I've raced against him in the kayak races on the Colorado. He's a darned good kayaker but we'll catch him. What's he wanted for?"

"It's a long story. I'll fill you in later. He's probably got a three or four hour head start on us. He's supposedly unarmed but let's play it safe. When we see him, just throttle back and let me talk to him from a distance."

"Okay, Manny. Have you been on the river before?"

"No. This is my first raft trip anywhere. It's something I've always wanted to do." He smiled. "But I wasn't expecting it to be part of a high-speed chase."

"We should catch up to him before he gets to the confluence," said Doug. "So don't worry. We won't have to chase him all the way through Cataract Canyon."

Rivera grinned. "I'm glad to hear that."

He sat in the front of the raft, his gaze fixed downriver. He began wondering what he would do when he spotted Petrov. By now, law enforcement personnel would be waiting at the Hite Crossing Bridge, the first road across the river. Petrov wouldn't be able to get past that point. But what if Petrov stopped somewhere between here and there and tried to escape through a side canyon? Because of his leg he would need some help. And Petrov had had time to make a call and arrange for help.

Rivera scanned both sides of the canyon and the river up ahead as far as he could see. So did Doug. Each time they passed a side canyon, they slowed down and inspected it. The side canyons were dry so if Petrov used one of them to escape, his abandoned kayak might be visible at the mouth of the canyon. Of course, Petrov could have hidden it in a clump of brush, or buried it in the sand, or sent it on its way downriver. Regardless, they would keep a sharp lookout.

Rivera enjoyed the cool breeze, the occasional blast of mist when the raft slapped the water, and the incredible scenery. The redrock canyon walls on each side of the river rose eight-hundred feet straight up to a ribbon of blue sky. The canyon was full of small birds, egrets, and ducks. Mule deer were a common sight on the flats. At one point, Doug pointed out a small herd of desert bighorn sheep on a rocky ledge.

After thirty minutes of looking at vertical canyon walls interrupted periodically by side canyons large and small, Rivera began wondering where he was. He asked Doug.

"I don't know exactly, Manny. I've been rafting the Green River for three years and I still have trouble telling one side canyon from another. I have a general idea of how far we've come but it's just a guesstimate. The problem is you can't see any landmarks like Cleopatra's

Chair or Elaterite Butte or Turk's Head from down here. Just the canyon walls. But I'd say we're a few miles north of The Maze. I can get out my GPS receiver and check if you want."

"No, no, I'm just curious. All the kayak races are in the Colorado River, so Petrov knows that canyon real well. But here on the Green, he's in foreign territory. If he was going to meet someone in one of these side canyons, I was just wondering how he would identify it. Of course, he might have a GPS receiver too. But, maybe not. Just thinking out loud."

Rivera noticed something written on the canyon wall up ahead. He pointed. "What's that?"

Doug throttled back and moved the raft closer to shore so Rivera could get a better view. There was an inscription chipped into the canyon wall. It read:

D. Julien
1836
3Mai.

It was accompanied by the outline of a boat.

"Have you ever heard of Denis Julien?"

"The name rings a bell. Wasn't he one of the early explorers in this area?"

"Right. Back in the eighteen-thirties and eighteen-forties. He was a French-American trapper. He left his inscription in several places. I believe there are seven others. I've seen one in Arches National Park and another in Cataract Canyon. Apparently he was one of the first human beings to make it through the rapids of Cataract Canyon. Did it in a wooden boat."

"Even before John Wesley Powell?"

"Yeah. Maybe Lake Powell should have been named Lake Julien."

Twenty more minutes passed. The red rock walls quietly glided by. Doug broke the silence. "Manny, if he stayed on the river, we should be getting pretty close to him about now."

Rivera nodded and focused his attention downriver.

39

AS THEY ROUNDED A bend in the river, Rivera spotted a red and white kayak a quarter-mile ahead. There was a man sitting in it, slumped over and motionless. The kayak was near the east river bank, slowly rotating in an eddy pool shaded by the cliffs.

They approached slowly. Rivera put his hand on his pistol, told Doug to stay low. He'd never shot anyone and hoped today would be no exception. He yelled out to the man. There was no response. Only the echoes of his voice from the massive canyon walls. They moved closer. Rivera called out a second time. Still no response. When they were about a hundred feet away, Rivera could see blood on the man's shoulder. They moved to within thirty feet. It was Petrov and it looked like he'd been shot.

Rivera jumped into the shallow pool and pulled the kayak onto the bank. He lifted Petrov from the boat and laid him down in a soft patch of sand. He checked for a pulse. Petrov was still alive.

"Doug, get on the satellite phone and call in the MedEvac helicopter. We need to get this man to the hospital."

"Already on it," was the reply. "They can set the chopper down on that sand bar we passed about a quarter-mile back." Doug checked his GPS receiver and read off the coordinates to the MedEvac operator.

Rivera patted down Petrov. He wasn't carrying a weapon. Rivera removed the life jacket and cut the man's shirt open with his pocketknife. The slug had entered Petrov's shoulder from the rear and did not exit. Rivera retrieved the first aid kit from the raft and began treating the wound as best he could. There wasn't much he could do except apply an antiseptic and try to stop the bleeding with gauze and tape. Petrov groaned and opened his eyes. Looked at Rivera. Then he shut them again.

After the bleeding was stanched, Rivera carefully carried Petrov to the raft. Then he inspected the kayak. It contained nothing of importance. He dragged it up onto the highest point on the bank and turned it upside down. That done, they set off upriver for the sandbar.

Twenty-five minutes later, Rivera could hear the thump-thump of the helicopter up the canyon. Soon it came into view. Rivera and Mather turned away and closed their eyes as the chopper landed on the sand-bar in a cloud of flying sand. Two medical technicians with a stretcher hopped off and trotted over to where Rivera was waiting. They checked the wounded man's dressing and strapped him onto the stretcher.

"Nice job treating the wound," one of them said. "Are you coming back with us?"

"Yes. This man is my prisoner." Rivera thanked Doug and said goodbye.

"Anytime, Manny."

Rivera followed the techs back to the chopper and soon they were in the air headed for the Moab Regional Hospital.

Late that afternoon, Rivera was sitting in Sheriff Bradshaw's office with the door closed. He'd just finished briefing Bradshaw on the details of the capture. They were both drinking coffee.

"Well, we've gotten the man wanted by the FBI. That should solve their problem. But we still don't have our killer," said Bradshaw.

"No, but I'll bet Petrov knows who the killer is. He's bound to be the one who hired him. Petrov is in the operating room now. The docs tell me he's going to be okay. I'll give him the night to recover and then question him in the morning. Maybe he'll be willing to give us the name of the shooter."

"Okay, Manny. But we'll need the FBI's permission to interview Petrov. I'll talk to Lisowski tonight."

"I heard the FBI already had a big press conference announcing the capture."

"Yep. National TV, newspaper reporters, the works. Lisowski made the announcement. Said they'd been tracking Petrov for years and finally trapped him in a remote canyon in Utah." Bradshaw was grinning as he spoke. "Toward the end of the conference, he did manage to acknowledge the assistance of local law enforcement personnel."

"Unbelievable," said Rivera.

"Better get used to it, Manny. It's the way they operate."

40

DIMITRI WAS SITTING ON the edge of his bed eating the breakfast tacos he'd bought at a tiny Mexican restaurant in Monticello. In a couple of hours, he would leave the motel and drive to the Hite Crossing Bridge as the boss had instructed him. Right now, he was watching an episode of *La Familia con Suerte* on the television in his room. An older man and a shapely young woman were arguing in Spanish. They were face-to-face, both talking in loud voices at the same time. Dimitri grinned throughout the show, pausing only to wolf down another taco.

The telephone rang. He thought about not answering it but it was probably the boss.

"Hello?"

"Dimitri, this is the boss. There's been a change of plans. Forget about the Hite Crossing Bridge. I just heard on the news about Boris. The Feds captured him and are holding him in the hospital in Moab. He was shot and wounded."

"How bad wound?"

"Not bad. He'll be okay. It wasn't you who shot him, was it, Dimitri?"

"No boss. I not supposed to go to the bridge until later today."

"Okay, okay. I know. Look Dimitri, I have a new job for you."

"Yes, boss."

"Go to the hospital early tomorrow morning. Find a way to get into Boris's room and kill him. He'll be guarded so you may have to disguise yourself as a hospital employee. Do whatever you have to do. But make sure you kill him."

"Yes, boss. What about computers?"

"If Boris had them when he was captured, the FBI has them now. That would cost us some money. But that's okay. We make lots more every day. Some of our operations will be compromised, so we'll have to make some changes in the way we do business. We'll adapt. If we're lucky, Boris dumped the computers in the river before he was captured."

* * *

Lisowski's face was red. He slapped his palm on the table. "I gave strict orders that Petrov was not to be shot. Now who the hell shot him?"

Sheriff Bradshaw looked around the conference room. The same people who attended the first meeting with the FBI Agent-In-Charge were present. Bradshaw noticed that everyone was seated in exactly the same seat as yesterday. There was silence in the room.

Lisowski persisted. "Well?" He looked around the room, his glance lingering on each deputy sheriff. "My men were covering the highways. It had to be someone covering the backcountry."

After a long moment, Bradshaw spoke. "Phil, Petrov was shot with a .30 caliber bullet. Most likely a hunting rifle. My deputies carry only Glocks and shotguns. I'm sure the same is true with Sheriff Zilic's deputies." He voice was deliberately calm.

Zilic nodded his head. "That's correct." Zilic's voice wasn't so calm.

"Well, I've heard that some rural deputies carry hunting rifles in their vehicles. Out of sight. Comes in handy out in the backcountry during the hunting season."

"There would be no reason for a deputy to shoot Petrov. If he made it through Cataract Canyon, we'd have just scooped him up at the Hite Crossing Bridge," said Bradshaw.

"Yeah, well just the same, I'm considering launching a full investigation. When the FBI gives orders, we expect them to be carried out." His face was now just a pale shade of pink. He took a sip of coffee. "As soon as the doctors tell us it's okay to move Petrov, we'll take him to a safe place and interrogate him. He's indicated he might cooperate with us in exchange for a plea bargain. He wants full immunity and protection. One last thing. We haven't been able to locate his two laptops. They weren't in his office, home, ranch, or vehicle. He probably dumped them in the river but let's keep an eye out for them anyway. The computers would give us a lot of leverage in striking a deal with him."

41

DIMITRI ENTERED THE HOSPITAL through an unlocked rear door on the loading dock. He located a utility closet, stepped inside, and turned on the light. Several green orderly uniforms were hanging from hooks on a clothes rack. He selected the largest and put it on over his clothing. He emerged from the closet, found a trash collection cart, and began pushing it down one of the hallways. It was very early Sunday morning and the halls were empty.

Dimitri was proud he was considered an effective and reliable hit man. His philosophy was to be bold and not hesitate even an instant. Stopping to rethink the risks or being overly cautious would make you stand out like a sore thumb. Just proceed directly to the target and do the job. Then calmly depart. That method of operation had always served him well. And that was exactly what he planned to do today.

Dimitri would know Boris's room because it would have a police guard sitting outside the door. On the first floor, he went down one hallway, then the next.

No police guard. He took the elevator to the second floor. He pushed the cart out and stopped, looking left then right. At the end of the hallway to the right, he saw a man in a dark suit sitting in a chair outside one of the rooms. He slowly proceeded in that direction. The guard was reading a magazine. He glanced at Dimitri approaching, then returned his attention to the magazine.

Dimitri stopped directly in front of the man. He nodded toward the door. "Trash pickup."

The guard stood up. "No one's allowed in this room."

Dimitri did his best to speak in a pleading voice. "Trash pickup my job. Only need trash can."

The man made a wry face and shook his head. "Just a minute. I'll get it for you. Wait here." He dropped the magazine on the chair.

The man turned and pushed open the door. Dimitri slammed the butt of his pistol into the back of the guard's head who fell into the room unconscious. Dimitri entered the room and closed the door. He went over to Boris's bed and shook him until he opened his eyes.

"Dimitri, what are you doing here?" But the expression on Boris's face said he already knew the answer to that question. And he looked too weak to resist.

Dimitri smiled. "The boss asked me to kill your father and I did." Boris's eyes widened. "Now he wants me to kill you." Boris started to say something, then fell silent, seemingly resigned to his fate. Dimitri raised his pistol, pointed it at Boris's head, and fired a single shot. He turned and left the room. He walked down the hallway away from the elevators and toward the stairs.

About halfway to the stairs, he heard a loud angry voice. "FBI. Freeze or I'll shoot."

Dimitri stopped and looked over his shoulder. It was the guard. He was leaning against the wall with one hand and pointing a pistol at Dimitri with the other. He appeared a bit groggy. Maybe too groggy to shoot straight. Dimitri's hand was still on his gun but the gun was in his pocket. He thought about turning and firing but he knew he was a lousy shot unless the target was a foot or two away. He put up his hands. "No shoot. Dimitri surrender."

42

SHERIFF BRADSHAW WAS SITTING at his desk finishing off the roast beef sandwich his wife Jill had made for him. Despite her pain, she still insisted on fixing his lunch like she always did. There was a knock on the door. Manny Rivera walked in and sat down. He put a file on Bradshaw's desk.

"We just got the results of the ballistics test on Dimitri's gun," said Rivera. "It was a match for the slugs that killed February Flanagan and William Reynolds. It was also a match for the slug found in Bart Winslow and, of course, the one that killed Boris Petrov. So I think we can close the books on the February Flanagan case and the murders which followed."

"Yeah. Good job, Manny. Now maybe things can start getting back to normal in Moab. And I'll be able to spend more time with Jill. Hopefully the mob element is gone from our little town, never to return. I just don't understand those people. How could Boris Petrov have ever expected to be happy? He must have been looking over his shoulder every day of his life.

And this fellow Dimitri was really messed up in the head. When he was arrested, all he wanted to know was whether he'd be able to watch television in prison. And whether they showed cartoons. And whether he could buy candy bars. There was not an iota of remorse or regret. He smiled like a child through the whole booking and interrogation process. Sociopaths like Dimitri scare me. They make me wonder why I ever got into this business."

"I know what you mean. And I like the idea of things in Moab getting back to normal. I had to cancel my date with Vivian last night. We were supposed to have dinner at the Sunset Grill. We've rescheduled it for tomorrow night."

"Great place. Jill and I used to go there about once a month. But now…" Bradshaw let the sentence trail off, then changed the subject. "We still have one remaining problem. A very irritating one. Phil Lisowski has called another meeting for one o'clock." He looked at his watch. "Thirty minutes from now. He wants to talk with Sheriff Zilic and me about Boris Petrov. Petrov's death means Lisowski won't get the information he wanted about the mob's operations. So now he's madder than ever about the shooting on the river. He thinks if Petrov hadn't been wounded and brought to the hospital, he'd still be alive and in FBI custody. And Lisowski would still be able to make a deal with him. He's certain one of our deputies is the culprit." He scratched his head.

"Jill was feeling a little better this morning. She wanted me to take her to church. Instead I have to listen to another Lisowski rant."

"Good luck with the meeting. I'm glad I don't have to be there. I couldn't take another minute with that guy."

The meeting took place in the conference room. Lisowski had brought another FBI agent with him to the meeting. A new face.

"Well, we got our man. But I wanted him alive." Lisowski spoke slowly and deliberately, poking the table with his index finger as he articulated each word. His eyes shifted back and forth between Bradshaw and Zilic. "I made that very clear. Someone ignored those instructions and shot Petrov anyway. And that cost us a load of intelligence on the mob's operations. That's a huge loss. And since we never found the computers, we don't have that source of intelligence either. We've come up completely empty intelligence-wise." He leaned forward, rested his forearms on the table, and folded his hands. "It had to be a deputy from either Grand County or San Juan County. You folks were staking out the backcountry. The state cops were on the highways and the city cops were in town. So were my men. It had to be a deputy sheriff. Gentlemen, I'm announcing a full investigation of the shooting incident on the river. We *will* get to the bottom of this. Agent Steve Tolliver here will be in charge." He motioned to his associate. "He's very good at this kind of investigation. I have every confidence he'll get to the bottom of it. I'm going back to Washington tomorrow morning. Agent Tolliver will keep me informed on a daily basis. That is all." He stood up and summarily marched out of the room, followed by Tolliver.

After they were gone, Bradshaw and Zilic went back to Bradshaw's office and sat down. Bradshaw asked his secretary to have Rivera join them, which he did. Rivera quietly closed the door behind him, and Bradshaw briefed him on what had taken place at the meeting. All three men sat with somewhat stunned expressions.

Zilic broke the silence. "I've worked with lots of FBI agents over the years, but never one like Lisowski. He's pure politics. Must feel right at home in Washington."

"I suppose they'll be wanting to search the vehicles and homes of each deputy for .30 caliber rifles. Test each one until they find the rogue deputy who shot Petrov," said Bradshaw with a smile. He shook his head. "I can't believe this is happening."

"If only we'd have found Petrov's computers," said Zilic. "That might have satisfied Lisowski. He'd have a load of intelligence their analysts could pore over. Now he has to return to Washington empty-handed. I suppose he'll have a tough time explaining to the brass how he let Petrov get killed." Zilic made a wry face. "Serves him right. He botched the whole thing."

Rivera spoke up. "It's really a good question, though. Dimitri didn't have a rifle in his Range Rover, so we can rule him out. And it wasn't a hunting accident. It was a deliberate shot. By an expert marksman. From the angle of entry, the shot had to come from the top of a bluff eight-hundred feet above the river. Someone took aim at the man in the kayak. Certainly it wasn't one of our people. There would be absolutely no reason for a deputy to do such a stupid thing, knowing how valuable Petrov's knowledge would be. Could it be we have a local terrorist we need to be worrying about?"

"A good question," said Bradshaw.

43

MANNY RIVERA SCANNED THE canyon walls as Doug Mather steered the motorized raft downriver from Mineral Bottom. Rivera had a hunch.

"Doug, thanks a lot for the ride."

"Can't think of a better way to spend a Sunday afternoon. What are we looking for?"

"After we arrested Dimitri, he sang like a bird. He didn't know much about the mob's operation, only that he worked for a man he'd never met. Didn't even know his name. He called him *the boss.* Said he thought he lived somewhere in Arizona, maybe Phoenix. Dimitri was just a well-paid hit man. Not too bright but he was very effective. There was one thing he told us that got me to thinking. He said Petrov told him that his two laptop computers were always in his possession wherever he went, so he must have had them when he left his ranch and drove back to Moab. Then he must have seen the FBI vehicles and started to run. He picked up his kayak and headed for the river. Chose the Green instead of the Colorado, probably because it was more remote.

"He launched his kayak and instinctively he would have taken the computers with him. They weren't in his vehicle and he didn't have them when we found him, so either he dumped them in the river where by now they'd be buried under the silt forever, or he hid them for later retrieval. It seems to me he would have hidden them."

"Why?"

"For several reasons. If he was captured and he still had the computers with him, he'd have less leverage in making a plea deal with the FBI. Without the computers, Petrov would be the sole source of information that the FBI could tap into. But if the FBI had possession of the computers and they contained critical information about the mob's finances and operations, maybe they wouldn't need Petrov's knowledge at all."

"That makes sense."

"There's another possibility. If Petrov had escaped down the river somehow and was rescued by his mob friends, the hidden computers would serve as an insurance policy on his life. He might have sensed his life was in danger and took precautions. And he was right, of course."

"So if the computers are hidden, how do we find them?"

"Petrov was very familiar with the Colorado River Canyon since that's where he and his kayaking friends had their races. But he wouldn't have been so familiar with the Green River Canyon. I remember thinking yesterday how the appearance of the canyon walls and side canyons all looked so similar. Miles and miles of them. After a while, it all runs together in your mind. The height of the canyon walls prevents anyone at river level from seeing any landmarks along the horizon. We didn't find a GPS receiver in Petrov's kayak, so if he did hide the computers, how would he ever find them again?"

"I think I know where you're going with this line of thought. And I think you might be right."

They continued several more miles downriver. It was another perfect October day, with a clear blue sky and temperatures in the mid-seventies. They came around a bend and Doug throttled back the engine and began edging the craft toward the shoreline. "There it is," Rivera said, pointing to the Denis Julien inscription on the canyon wall. "The only truly unique location marker in the river canyon." They jumped onto the bank and pulled the end of the raft up onto the sand. Doug secured it with a rope tied to a tamarisk.

Rivera approached the inscription noting several sets of footprints in the area, some with shoes, some barefoot. Tourists. "He wouldn't have hidden it right here where people stop to see the inscription," he said. "This sand bar is about four hundred yards long. He probably hid the computers some distance away from the inscription so they wouldn't be accidentally discovered. I'm guessing they would be up high, maybe in a crack in the canyon wall, somewhere behind a stand of bushes."

"Sounds right. They'd have to be above the high-water mark so the spring snowmelt wouldn't damage them."

Rivera looked up and down the river. "Let's head downriver from here. If we don't find them, we'll try upriver. I doubt there will be footprints in the sand. A guy with his brains would have brushed them out. And then the wind in this canyon would have wiped away the brush marks."

They set off to the south, side-by-side, working their way through the brush and scanning up and down the canyon wall. The brush was thick and in some places thorny, so the going was slow. They checked each crack in the wall and inspected each rock pile along the base of the wall. After an hour of searching, they completed the downriver portion of the inspection. They returned to the starting point and repeated the process along the upriver segment. They found nothing. They returned to the raft and sat down in the sand to rest.

Rivera looked at the dozens of scratches on his arms. "I guess my theory was wrong."

Doug had retrieved a tube of antiseptic ointment from the first aid kit in the raft and was applying it to a cut on his wrist. "Well, it was a good thought,

Manny. Now, where else could Petrov have hidden the computers?"

Rivera shrugged. "Good question." He stood up and walked back to the Denis Julien inscription. Looked around. He thought about the footprints in the sand. They might have given Petrov reason to pause and rethink his plan. He wouldn't want the computers accidentally found by tourists on the river. But the Julien inscription was such a perfect marker. What would Petrov have done? Rivera looked across to the other side of the river. "Say, Doug, let's motor across the river and search the west bank."

Thirty minutes later, Rivera was holding the waterproof case in his hands. It contained the two computers he'd seen in Williams's office. He'd found them in a crack in the canyon wall behind a thick stand of tamarisk. They were up high, and several loose rocks had been shoved into the crack to conceal the package.

Late that afternoon, Sheriff Bradshaw stuck his head into Rivera's office. "I presented the computers to Phil Lisowski," a smiling Bradshaw said. "He appreciated what you did very much. Even seemed cordial. He said to tell you thanks and nice job."

"Did he call off the investigation into who shot Petrov?"

"Absolutely not. The man's a stubborn bulldog. He seriously wants to hang whoever disobeyed his orders.

He did have one request though. He asked if you would go back to the Winslow residence and search Bart Winslow's cabin. They've been analyzing the contents of his computer and were wondering if there were any related materials there. Notebooks, disks, thumb drives, yellow stickies with passwords written on them, so forth. They're especially interested in passwords. Since Mr. and Mrs. Winslow know you, Lisowski thought it would be better if you went. I agree with him."

44

MANNY RIVERA KNOCKED ON the door of the Winslow residence and waited. Henry Winslow answered the door. He looked tired and distraught.

"I'm sorry to trouble you, Henry. I need to visit Bart's cabin again. The FBI requested that I pick up some additional items for their investigation."

"Sure, Manny. No problem," he said with an expressionless face. He handed him his key ring.

Rivera walked through the house. As he passed the kitchen he caught a glimpse of Mrs. Winslow slicing potatoes on a cutting board. Her eyes were red, her hair uncombed. She looked like she'd aged ten years. She didn't look up. He continued out the back door, across the yard, and into the cabin.

The radio in the cabin was still on. Paul Winter's *Wolf Eyes* was playing. Rivera quickly gathered up all the items from Bart's desk he thought might possibly be pertinent to the FBI's investigation. There were notebooks, loose sheets of paper with printed notes, a box containing about a dozen labeled disks and several thumb drives. He also peeled several yellow Post-It notes off the wall behind the desk. Each had handwritten notations that Rivera guessed might be passwords. He left the cabin and re-entered the house. As he passed Henry's office, he saw him sitting there behind the desk. He stuck his head in the office to say goodbye.

"I'm leaving now. Thank you, Henry." He returned the key ring.

"Okay, Manny."

Rivera noticed the same music he heard in Bart's cabin was playing in Henry's office. He glanced at the source and saw that it was coming from the intercom connected to the cabin. The intercom must have been left on by Bart and never turned off. It was at that instant Rivera realized the man who had shot Boris Petrov on the river was Henry Winslow. He quickly replayed the sequence of events of the last few days through his mind. It all fit. Rivera made a decision he hoped was the right thing to do.

"Henry, before I go I wanted to mention one thing to you. In confidence."

Henry raised his eyebrows.

"The FBI is initiating an investigation into who shot Boris Petrov on the Green River. They wanted Petrov alive because he had a lot of information on mob activities. I think they're on a wild goose chase. It was probably just a hunting accident. But if it was me who shot him, I'd hide the rifle that I used and keep it hidden for five or ten years."

Henry sat there for a long moment, wide-eyed and speechless. Finally he stood up and walked over to Rivera. He extended his hand. "Thank you for everything."

Rivera thought about Henry Winslow as he drove back to the office. He was a good man who'd been crushed by the loss of two sons. He must have been sitting in his office when Rivera called Emmett Mitchell from Bart's cabin. He'd heard Rivera say that Boris Petrov, alias Richard Meriwether Williams, was responsible for Bart's murder. Then, later in the day, Rivera had called Sheriff Bradshaw from the radio in his vehicle since the batteries in his cell phone were dead. A breach of protocol, but there was nothing else Rivera could have done at the time. He had to inform Bradshaw that Petrov was escaping in a red and white kayak down the Green River. That call was also heard by Henry Winslow over the police scanner he had in his office. Henry heard the discussion about how long it would be before they could arrange for a raft to make the chase, so he must have figured Petrov stood a good chance of escaping. He also figured there was something he could do about it. As an experienced hunter and a backcountry expert, Henry made his way to a down-river bluff overlooking the Green River and waited. It was a difficult shot, shooting down eight-hundred feet. But Henry was able to do it. Rivera wondered if Henry intended only to wound Petrov so he couldn't paddle, or if he meant to kill him. He decided he really didn't want to know the answer to that question.

The FBI would conduct its investigation and if it occurred to them to check Henry's collection of rifles they would find nothing incriminating. The hell with Lisowski and his investigation. Henry Winslow and his wife already had more than their share of trouble in life.

45

A NARROW BAND of dark purple clouds hung low in the western sky, backlit by an iridescent orange-pink afterglow which outlined the horizon. Just above the clouds, Venus was glowing brightly in a light blue sky. A candle flickered on their table next to the window at the Sunset Grill. Manny Rivera felt relaxed for the first time in a week.

Vivian Ramos reached across the table and touched his hand. "Well, we finally made it."

"Finally," He smiled and raised his wineglass. "Here's to you. Thanks for waiting for me." He could hardly take his eyes off her. She was wearing a short beige dress which accentuated her curves and her dark hair was pulled straight back to a pearl clip before falling to her shoulders.

They sipped their wine quietly for a few moments, looking at each other, then glancing at the view to the west, then back at each other. It was one of those perfect evenings.

"A lot has happened in Moab the past few days. Everyone in town is talking about how you broke the February Flanagan case. Is everything wrapped up now?" Vivian asked.

"Pretty much. At least on our end of it. The FBI is still chasing down the other false identities Bart created. I expect there will be more arrests. And the information on Boris's computers should help them put a dent in organized crime."

The waiter came and took their dinner order. Vivian ordered grilled salmon with capers, Manny a medium-rare filet.

"Did you know February Flanagan?" she asked.

"No, but I wish I had. He disappeared shortly after I moved to Moab. I'd heard a little about him back then but never got to meet him. He must have had an amazing mind. I think I could have learned a lot from him about how to conduct an investigation."

"It seems to me you did pretty well on your own. And don't forget, you finished his investigation for him."

Rivera reflected on that. Nodded. "I hadn't thought of it that way."

"Beatrice, one of the nurses I work with at the hospital, called and told me about a conversation she had with Boris in his room about an hour before he was killed."

"Really? What'd she say?"

"She's an older woman, kind of a grandmotherly figure. She said Boris was full of regret about what he'd done with his life. He missed Claire and needed her more than ever. The FBI wouldn't let Boris use the phone to make any calls. So he asked Beatrice to do it. She called but Claire said she wouldn't come. When she'd heard what had happened and who her husband really was, she didn't want to see him again. She was deeply hurt and embarrassed. Then, just after the shooting, Claire was seen rushing into the hospital. I guess she'd had a change of heart, but it was too late."

Rivera thought that over. "My grandfather told me something years ago when I was just a teenager, maybe fourteen years old. He said life is fundamentally a long series of decisions. You make them every day. And all it takes is one bad decision to ruin your life. That always stuck with me. How easy it is to mess up a life."

Vivian was silent, attentive, beautiful.

Rivera continued. "I saw this movie once. There was a philosopher in the story. He had a foreign accent. German, maybe. He said, 'We are the sum total of the decisions we make in life.' I think that summarizes everything pretty well. William Reynolds decided to try to become a famous journalist by stealing Flanagan's stories. Bart Winslow decided it was okay to steal identities and sell them. Boris Petrov decided to work for the mob after he graduated from college. Their decisions did not lead to happiness, only regret and ultimately death." He paused, considered that. "I guess, in a way, we *become* our decisions."

The waiter brought their meals. They ate quietly, Rivera thinking how unromantic and boring his conversation had been. Why had he gone on and on about this abstract subject of decision making and its impact on one's life. And why choose a time like this, sitting here with a beautiful woman, eating a fabulous meal, and watching day turn to night in a most extraordinary way. It was time to quit philosophizing and get back to living.

"Vivian, how would you like to take a moonlight drive through Arches National Park after dinner?"

She smiled. "I'd like that."

Author's Note

The Denis Julien inscription described in Chapter 38 is actually located at the top of a talus slope in Hell Roaring Canyon, some 750 feet up-canyon from the Green River. I took the liberty of changing its location to a canyon wall on the Green River to provide Manny Rivera a unique position marker on the river.

The Bart Winslow computer hacking attacks are purely figments of my imagination. I have no personal knowledge of the Utah Office of Vital Statistics computer system.

Made in the USA
San Bernardino, CA
07 September 2019